Look for More Titles by Cassandra Chandler

The White Stag

Court of the Yuletide Fae
Book Two

Cassandra Chandler

Copyright Page

You are a good person! You know that stealing is wrong. Remember, eBooks can't be shared or given away. It's against copyright law. So don't download books you haven't paid for or upload books in ways other people can access for free. That would be stealing.
And you're better than that.

The White Stag
Court of the Yuletide Fae, Book Two
Copyright © 2023 by Cassandra Chandler
Print ISBN: 978-1-945702-15-0
Digital ISBN: 978-1-945702-14-3

First eBook edition: January 2023
First print edition: January 2023
10 9 8 7 6 5 4 3 2 1

cassandra-chandler.com
P.O. Box 91
Mission, Kansas 66201

Dedication

For S.E. Smith, whose generous heart and loving nature inspires me every day.

Don't miss out on any of the magic.
Subscribe to Cassandra Chandler's newsletter at
cassandra-chandler.com!

Chapter One

The lights from the Christmas tree cast rainbow patterns on the polished oak of the cabin walls. Sylvia pulled her blanket closer around her shoulders as she stared at them. She should probably take the decorations down, since it was almost New Year's, but they were a reminder that she had made it through her first Christmas Day as a single woman in years, even if she'd spent it at the same cabin where she and her ex, David, had always celebrated.

He had accused her of claiming the cabin out of spite, but she honestly just loved the place. The outside of the dwelling looked rustic, with rough-hewn timbers, but inside, the walls were smooth with panels stained to bring out the wood's rich golden hue. A giant fireplace made of natural stone took up most of one corner of the cabin, the multi-hued granite absorbing heat from the fire and keeping the cabin cozy on all but the most frigid days.

The front door had beautiful stained glass in rich purples, reds, and greens, depicting a forest scene that Sylvia had designed herself. Though there weren't too many other windows, they were placed to make the most of what natural light could filter into the cabin though the lush forest outside. The trees weren't thick enough around the cabin to block the solar panels that gave her electricity or to keep rainwater from being collected in the clever reservoir the architect had built into the cabin's design, but they still left her with a feeling of being embraced by nature.

She gazed at the great room that was both comfortingly familiar and achingly empty. How many nights had she spent in the loft staring out the highest windows at the stars peeking through the canopy beyond? How many hours had she spent in the open kitchen, cooking while their friends sat at the stools surrounding the island that sectioned off that space from the rest of the great room?

Now it was just her. She was grateful that they hadn't had kids or pets. That would have made their already painful divorce so much worse. He could have the house in the city and his fancy car—and their friends, most of whom he'd been sleeping with, it turned out. At least, the female ones. The guys had all apparently known about his conquests and cheered him on from the sidelines.

All Sylvia really wanted was this cabin and everything in it—the designs she had made and the items she selected to make it feel like a home. All she needed was the beautiful forest surrounding it, teeming with wildlife. The nearest neighbor was miles away. It had been a draw at first, but she had to admit she was now getting a little lonely. And cold.

She reluctantly let the blanket fall to the couch, then went to the fire and added a few more logs. While they caught, she hurried upstairs to get more blankets and pillows. This was going to be a night for sleeping in front of the fire, it seemed. She looked out the window in the loft area, barely able to make out the trees through the driving snow in the fading light. They had definitely received their white Christmas—and then some.

She shivered as the cold hit her, then grabbed all the blankets that were piled on the bed and pulled them into her arms, along with several pillows. She could barely see the steps as she made her way back downstairs. At least her armful of fluff would cushion her landing if she tripped. When she made it to the fireplace, she dropped everything on the plush faux fur rug in front of the safety screen, then grabbed the poker to stir up the blaze.

She had just finished banking the fire when a tremendous crash reverberated through her cabin. Pictures shook on the walls and the many bookshelves tilted back and forth precariously. She fell backwards, luckily landing on her blanket pile.

"What the heck was that?"

It had almost sounded like an explosion. She quickly put the poker back in its place and set the fire screen in front of the hearth to keep the blaze she'd worked up safely behind it. She had really been looking forward to cozying up with her pile of blankets and pillows. Hopefully, whatever this was, she'd be able to proceed with her evening as planned, after investigating.

She ran to the front door and grabbed her coat, hat, and gloves. Even a few minutes outside would freeze her solid, and she wasn't in the mood to turn into a snow person. She pulled everything on in record time, then grabbed her go-bag and hurried outside, shutting the door behind her as quickly as she could to keep the warmth of the cabin inside.

Dusk was falling over the forest, but she still had enough light to see. The large flakes of snow coming down in a steady stream worried her a lot more than the darkness. She grabbed the emergency sled she kept by the door, just in case she needed it, and headed toward the sound of the crash. The crunch of snow beneath her feet was the only sound in the forest. All the wildlife had long since hunkered down for the storm, and the snow itself muted any ambient noise.

Before too long, evidence of… something began to show around her. The trees above had broken branches and piles of snow and pine needles beneath where everything that had been stuck to their limbs had been dislodged. It was almost like a meteor had come through. Bits of broken twigs and needles dotted the ground, already being covered by the falling snow.

"That's not good," she said. "Then again, neither is talking to myself constantly." She'd gotten into the habit after staying in the cabin alone for so long.

Maybe she was about to have an encounter with little green men. As long as there wasn't any probing involved, she'd be fine with making new friends. Heck, if the guy looked like the sexy aliens on the covers of some of those Scifi Romances she'd seen at the bookstore last time she went into town, she might not mind a little probing.

"I really have been alone too long."

She checked her GPS to make sure it was still working and she could find her way back to the cabin even after dark, then trudged deeper into the forest. More damage led the way for her. Whole trees had been felled. Her meteor theory was gaining ground. She skidded down an incline, pausing in a level spot that seemed to be the edge of the event horizon.

The light was fading, but she could still see well enough. Even better, the area was slightly shielded from the heavy snow. Scanning her surroundings, all she saw was white drifts punctuated by the occasional branch sticking through them. What could have caused all this damage, though? Had it already been covered in snow?

"Well, that was a waste," she said. Hopefully, the fire would still be burning nice and hot when she returned to the cabin. At least it hadn't taken too much time.

A sudden movement in her periphery caught her eye

and she froze. It wasn't the wind or snow. One of the branches had moved. She was sure of it. She should just turn around and keep heading back to her cabin and leave things be, but what if it was some animal that had been hurt when whatever this was had happened?

"Dangit." Cautiously, she made her way closer to the branch.

It stirred again as she grew closer. The way the branch had grown didn't look quite right. She wasn't sure what was off about what she was seeing until she was almost on top of it and realized that it wasn't a branch at all. It was an antler. An antler attached to the biggest, most beautiful stag she had ever seen.

His coat was completely white, blending in almost perfectly with the snow covering his body. The antlers caught the light oddly, gleaming like gold in the fading sun. They were also caught in a bunch of other branches and debris. It almost looked like the poor thing had crashed through the trees.

"Oh boy," she said. "You look like you're in a predicament."

She glanced up at the trees and froze. Standing right next to the stag, she could clearly see the line of damage that led straight to him. But it started at the tops of the trees. It started in the sky, as if *he'd* been the meteor.

"Okay, this is very weird."

She turned back to him and gasped. As the sunlight

faded even more, she could clearly see that his eyes were glowing, casting a soft gold light on the snow in front of him. Weren't there legends about a white stag? Like, if you caught him, he had to grant you a wish? There were so many things Sylvia would wish for. World peace—could he manage that? Happy homes for children and honestly everyone who needed them. Enough money to try to make a difference in the world, if he couldn't grant wishes that big.

He let out a sigh and looked up at her, his eyes filled with such sadness. Who gave a crap about wishes? This being—whatever he was—needed her help. She had to focus. They had already lost almost all their daylight.

"Sorry," she said. "This is kind of a new experience for me."

But only kind of. She had rescued animals and even people before. That's why she had the sled. It was big enough for a person, but she wasn't sure about the stag. She started digging out the snow around him, sweeping it away with her gloved hands. The snow darkened as she did. Had he stirred up some dirt as he fell? That didn't make sense. The ground was frozen.

Cautiously, she dusted the snow away from his body. She hissed in a breath as she saw four long gashes marring his white coat from his neck down to his shoulder. They weren't bleeding anymore, but they looked painful and deep. She reached out to gingerly touch the skin around

7

the area. The stag didn't flinch, but he watched her with wary eyes.

"I promise I won't hurt you," she said. She peered more closely at the injury. "What did you face off with? A giant grizzly?"

The stag closed his eyes, his head lowering as much as it could with all the debris restraining his antlers. How was she ever going to get him out of this? Now that she had cleared some of the snow from around him, she could see a large branch that was way too heavy for her to move— and the snow was still coming down. She would need a chainsaw to get him out of this and a tent or awning to keep the area clear while she worked. Even if she did get him free, he wouldn't fit on her sled. He was at least twice the size of any stag she'd ever seen.

"I don't know what to do," she said, resting one hand on his chest and the other on his antlers. "You're so tangled up, it'll take me hours to free you. Not that I'm not going to try," she quickly added. "I won't give up on you. I just… I wish I could help you more right now."

The antler she was holding onto warmed against her glove. She gasped and tried to pull away, but her hand was frozen in place. Not from the cold, but from something else. The antler glowed bright gold, the light was spreading over the stag and illuminating his entire body. He put off so much warmth, the snow around them melted.

She squinted against the brightness he was putting off,

trying to see what was happening. It looked as though his entire body was turning into pure light. She finally had to close her eyes against it, but she could feel him rippling and shifting under her hands. The antler she was stuck to shrank and flattened, the shape of his chest changed as it heaved with quick breaths. She heard him take in a huge gasp, like someone surfacing from water after too long below, and opened her eyes.

The most beautiful man she had ever seen was sprawled before her on the ground. His hair was pitch black, shorter on the sides than the top. Dark stubble coated his jaw. His eyebrows were also dark and strong, resting above thick lashes that surrounded amber-gold eyes. His soft lips were parted as he took in deep breaths.

Her scrutiny strayed over the rest of him, her eyes widening the more she saw. Broad shoulders and sculpted chest, rows of abs stacked on each other, muscled thighs and in between… Goosebumps raced along her skin, and not because of the cold. In fact, she was starting to feel quite warm—in certain places. Her eyes had to be popping out of her head. He was beyond perfect.

No one can be this hot.

Sylvia shook herself as she noticed four angry red lines that ran from his neck down across one shoulder. His wounds had healed incredibly, but they were still there. Whoever—whatever—this guy was, he needed her help, not for her to be lusting after him. And hadn't he just been a deer? Unless she had hallucinated that whole thing. That would make more sense, but she couldn't bring herself to believe it. No, this guy was some kind of… deer shifter. Yeah, that made sense. Like in the Paranormal Romances she'd been devouring since she had arrived at the cabin.

He was a super-hot deer shifter and she was going to plop him on her sled and take her back to her cabin. Where she would be respectful of his boundaries and not lust after him. Not at all.

Yeah, good luck with that.

Chapter Two

How was he so cold? Suddenly, transforming himself into a human didn't seem like such a good idea. He wasn't even sure how he could change back. All he knew was that the Krampus was hunting him, and this human had given him the perfect opportunity to escape. The Krampus was after the White Stag not... this human guy.

"C-c-cold," he stammered.

"You can talk? Great." The woman pulled a large orange sled alongside him. "Can you understand me?"

He nodded, still getting his bearings in this new form. Everything around them was so dim and white. The air was thick with falling flakes, obscuring both his vision and hearing.

"That'll make this a lot easier," she said. She pulled off her backpack and opened it, getting out a shiny silver packet from inside. With a shake, it unfolded into a blanket that she draped over him. "I need you to get on this sled so I can get you back to my shelter. Okay?"

He nodded again. The woman helped him roll onto the sled, which was somehow even colder than the ground. He hissed in a breath, curling himself up in a ball to try to stay warm.

"I need you to lay straight," she said. "I'm sorry the sled is so cold. The blanket should help with that."

He let her straighten his legs and then she tucked the blanket around him. It helped, but he still shivered violently. How could he become so cold so quickly? How did humans survive like this? He felt as though he'd never be warm again. The woman stared at him with a grim expression, then shook her head.

"This is going to suck," the woman said, but she seemed to be talking to herself.

She took off the long, thick coat she wore, then draped it over him. His body desperately soaked in the warmth stored in it—*her* warmth. But now, she would be the one who was freezing. He wanted to say something, to object, but his jaw was clenched shut from the cold. Once her coat was in place, she quickly pulled straps from the sled and secured him to it, then hefted her backpack onto her shoulders again. There were two longer straps attached to the top of the sled above his head. She looped them around herself and started pulling him through the snow. He managed to let out a laugh at the absurdity of it.

"What's so funny?" she said, grunting as she carted him up a steep incline.

Through chattering teeth, he forced out, "Y-you pulling me. D-don't humans usually use animals to p-pull them around in the snow?"

"Last I checked, you were a dude," Sylvia said.

He laughed again. "I g-guess so. I'm still ad-djusting to it."

"So, you're not a shifter then?"

"No. I'm j-just the White Stag. At least, I *w-was* the White Stag." His chest constricted. He didn't know what he was now or how to change back. At least the Krampus would leave him alone. In this form, there would be no granting wishes.

"What do I call you?" she asked, her voice winded.

"I don't c-care."

"Okay." She was quiet for a few moments, then said, "How about Buck?"

"Don't c-call me that."

"I thought you didn't care what I called you."

"That was before I knew you were thinking of calling me B-buck."

She snickered, the sound warming him somehow, and he smiled. She didn't seem like someone who laughed often. He wondered why and how else he might make her laugh. As a being who granted wishes, making others happy was something he truly enjoyed, as long as their wishes weren't harmful. Unfortunately, that was rarer than he would have liked.

A wave of sensation swept over him, his stomach tightened and his heart was beating faster. She had been given a wish, and she used it to help him. *Him.* Was that on purpose, or did she not know the meaning of capturing the White Stag? In all his time, he'd met many giving souls, but never one who thought of him. Some of the biting chill dissipated at the thought.

The sled paused for a moment. Now that he wasn't on the verge of freezing himself, he wondered how she was faring. She had given him her coat. Humans didn't have thick pelts or magic to keep them safe in the cold. What had she been thinking?

"Are you okay?" he asked, glad to find that his teeth had stopped chattering.

"Yeah, just adjusting the s-straps."

"Take back your coat," he said.

"No t-time. We're almost there."

He tried to move his arms to loosen the coat and give it to her, but she had strapped him in so tightly, he couldn't move. Panic reared up in him. He hated feeling trapped. It was like the many times he'd been captured as people sought him out for wishes. He closed his eyes and took slow breaths, the cold air burning his nostrils as he calmed himself. The chill passed from his lungs through his body, making him shiver harder again. Just how muted was his magic in this form?

Reaching out with what magic he had left, he found he could still sense the woman's heart. Warmth immediately suffused him and he gasped in a breath, struck first by her single-minded purpose and then by the intensity of her desire to help him. That was truly all she wanted in this moment, all she had wanted since finding him. In her heart, he was a being who needed help that she could offer. There was no question, no doubt, no glimpse of hesitation that she should give him that help. It was at the very core of her nature.

The sled started to move again. She made a few grunting noises, but the trees above him passed more quickly. Aside from the crunch of snow beneath her feet, all he could hear was her heavy breaths. The light was almost gone, and with it the last of the sun's warmth—what little of it there was. He tried to reach out with his magic to warm her, to ease her path, but felt a resistance between him and that aspect of his power that he couldn't pierce.

"Let me walk," he said. "I'm getting some of my strength back."

"You're still naked," she huffed. "We'll be lucky enough if you don't have frostbite by the time we get there. Oh, I see it. The cabin's just ahead. Hang on."

What did she mean by that? How was he supposed to hang on to anything when she had him wrapped up tighter than a caterpillar in a cocoon? She picked up speed, the sled moving fast enough to worry him a little. She had given him her wish, though. And her coat. She was risking her own wellbeing to help him. Beyond her actions, he had seen her heart. He knew he could trust her.

"Gonna get bumpy," she said.

"What?"

The sled suddenly angled upwards, a series of thumping sounds matching the sled being jostled as she dragged it up a short flight of stairs. She paused for a moment, then beautiful gold light and warmth washed over him. She dragged the sled inside the shelter and slammed the door shut behind her.

Thank the Gods that part is over.

Except the sled started to move again. It scraped across a wooden floor as she pulled him further into the cabin. From his limited vantage point, he could tell the place was still decorated for Christmas. He loved it when people left their decorations up after the holiday. It made the darkness of winter so much cheerier.

He still couldn't believe that the Krampus had been hunting him since just after Christmas day, the horrible wish in his heart reaching out with claws as sharp as the ones he had used to try to grapple with the White Stag. The Lord of Endless Snow, or just Snow, as Krampus was known in the Yuletide Kingdom, was supposed to gather tribute for the Winter Queen on Christmas—in the form of 'naughty' children who he claimed for her. Krampus was supposed to stick around and help them settle in after they had arrived. What was he doing hunting down the White Stag instead?

The Stag was part of the Yuletide Court, but he was considered a free agent. He had always felt more of an affinity for Lord Kringle than the Winter Queen, focusing on joy wherever he could. Many of the people who caught the Stag wished for things that he couldn't bear to grant, and he could sense that the Krampus's wish, whatever it was, would be among them. The White Stag had become wily over the millennia, learning to twist those wishes against the few who managed to catch him. No one had ever wished for something as straightforward as, 'I wish I could help you.'

And this woman *was* helping him, more than anyone ever had in his long existence. She was backing up her wish with action, was willing to work to make it come true. She had sacrificed for him without thought for herself, without hesitation. He could see in her heart the goodness there. And also a recent pain.

She thumped her feet, then removed her gloves and hat and tossed them out of his line of sight. From the sound of it, her boots followed shortly after, landing heavily on the floor near the door. She bent over him, undoing the straps with shaking, bloodless fingers.

"Sorry," she said. "I think I've gone a bit numb myself."

"It's okay," he said.

"Lucky for you, I just built up the fire and brought down a stack of blankets."

She leapt over him, toward the main source of warmth in the room. From the flickering lights on the ceiling, that must be the fireplace. He heard fabric rustling, then the sled shifted again. Her face appeared above him, his first good look at her.

Warm brown eyes stared intently at the straps as she worked to loosen them. Her hair was bright red, a complete mess from the snow and wearing her hat. She had a small, pert nose, round face, and full lips. He had the oddest urge to reach out and brush his fingertips over them, but his arms were still pinned to his sides.

"Dangit," she said. "Oh, here it goes."

She undid one strap, then another. Each one calmed him. She could have held him prisoner and demanded more wishes. That had happened before, too, but the Stag could grant only one wish per person. She had used hers. He wondered if she would mind.

The moment he was free, she took her coat from him and threw it aside. He was about to thank her when she hooked her fingers on the edge of the sled and flipped it over, dumping him onto a mix of blankets, pillows, and a thick faux fur rug. He let out a yelp that was muffled as she folded an immense pile of blankets over him. The weight of them was so much that he could barely breathe, but at least he was getting warmer.

The woman paced back and forth in front of the fire, rubbing her hands together. She looked like she was freezing. Her pantlegs were soaked through, as well as her shirt and the ends of her long hair. She hugged herself, patting her arms as if trying to restore feeling to them.

"What's your name?" he asked.

She stopped, eyeing him warily. That pain he had sensed earlier was rising up in her, mixed with a heavy dose of mistrust.

"It's okay," he said. "I'm not the kind of fairy that uses names against people."

She pinched her lips together, their corners lifting slightly. Was she about to laugh again? He wondered how he could push her over the edge into that lovely sound.

"But you *are* a fairy?" she said.

"I am."

"Never seen a fairy look like this before," she muttered.

He laughed and she froze again, eyes wide.

"Sorry, I'm not used to company," she said. "I've gotten into the habit of talking to myself. It weakens the filters."

"Your name," he said gently. "Please."

She hesitated for another beat, then said, "Sylvia."

He smiled. "Well, Sylvia, I'm not the only one on the verge of freezing. You need to get out of those wet clothes and get yourself warm."

He lifted the edge of the blankets. As he did, her eyes grew even wider, till he could see the whites all around them. She shook her head and took a step back. Was she afraid of him?

"I don't want you to be distressed because of helping me," he said. "I promise, I won't hurt you."

She snorted and murmured, "I've heard that one before." She snapped her mouth shut, glaring at him as if she expected a retort. When he didn't respond, she finally said, "Don't look."

He remembered that humans had issues with being seen naked and nodded, covering his eyes with his hands. The soft sound of her clothing moving over her skin made a strange sensation sweep over his own. It was probably just the cold.

More of the odd tingling covered him as he felt her shimmy under the covers behind him. He had the strongest urge to turn around and wrap his arms around her, but didn't think she would like that. Perhaps she had her own fears of being trapped. He let the blankets drop as she settled next to him, content to bask in the warmth of the fire and of the intriguing woman who had rescued him.

Chapter Three

Isolation had finally driven her mad. Sylvia's stubborn insistence on staying in the cabin was coming back to bite her. How else could she explain the events of the last hour? It had to be some kind of delusion or hallucination. At least it was a gorgeous hallucination. She only wished she wasn't so cold.

Another bout of shivers wracked her body. The guy craned his neck over his shoulder to look at her, his brow furrowing. She had hunkered down under the covers as much as she could, but she didn't seem to have any heat left to trap. At this rate, she was going to go into shock or become hypothermic or something. She should have packed two thermal blankets in her emergency bag.

"You're freezing," he said, rolling over to face her.

"You are t-too." Her teeth wouldn't stop chattering.

"I'm better, thanks to you."

He shimmied under the blankets, getting closer. She wanted to pull away, but when he lifted the covers separating them and his glorious heat rolled her way, she instinctively shifted toward him. He wrapped his muscled arms around her and pulled her close. Then closer.

Her heart started to pound as he lifted himself on his elbows and rose over her. He was naked and she was just in her underwear and a sports bra. What was he planning to do?

What wouldn't I encourage him to do?

Where the heck had that come from? She hadn't been with a man since leaving her husband a year ago—and she wasn't even sure this guy was a man. He had all the right parts in all the right places, but he had been a deer not long ago. A magical deer, but still.

"What are you d-doing?" she forced herself to ask.

"Moving you closer to the fire."

She shook her head. "N-no, you n-need if more than I d-do."

"I'm immortal," he said. "The cold couldn't kill me."

"N-now you tell me," she muttered.

He smiled gently, using the arm that was still beneath her to pull her closer to the fireplace. Once she was where he had just been—luxuriating in the warmth of the blankets in that spot—he settled in right behind her, his body pressed to hers. She would have protested, but he was so warm. He must be magic to have recovered so quickly. Besides, he felt too good tucked up next to her for her to resist.

His arm was beneath her head so that she was using his bicep as a pillow. Her ex would already be complaining about her big head pinching his arm and putting it to sleep. Instead, this guy was tucking the blankets around her body to trap every bit of warmth he could. When he was satisfied, he draped his other arm over her stomach, pulling her tight against his body.

There was no trace of arousal poking at her backside, which was a relief. Her cheeks prickled as she realized it was a disappointment as well. She had definitely been alone too long. She shouldn't be letting herself think such things about him. He made it all too easy, though, as he held her against his firm chest, sharing his warmth with her. Immortal or not, he had been through an ordeal.

"What happened to you?" she asked, trying to distract herself.

"The usual. People hunting me."

"Do they usually run you down with bears?"

His chest stilled as he held his breath a moment, his arms tensing around her. Slowly, he relaxed. His voice was guarded as he said, "You saw the claw marks."

She nodded. "Looked like a grizzly based on the spread. A huge one at that."

"Are you a hunter?"

She snorted. "Hardly. I used to want to be a vet tech."

"What happened?"

"I got married." She shrugged, then bunched herself deeper into the covers.

"Why would that make you stop wanting to be a vet

tech?"

"I just—" She let out an exasperated sound. "We're not talking about me. We're talking about you."

"O…kay."

"So, it was a bear?" she prompted.

"A polar bear."

"Wow."

She could imagine all too easily the white stag and the white bear battling it out. The stag wouldn't stand a chance. But it wasn't a normal fight. The stag had fallen from the sky—and not straight down. They hadn't been running around on a cloud or some celestial landscape. From the angle and trajectory, their fight had involved flying.

"So, it could fly, too?" she asked.

Again, he stiffened. "How do you know that?"

"The trees." She sniffed, her nose finally starting to thaw. "They were broken on the tops at an angle. I thought I was tracking down a meteor at first."

"If only."

She wasn't sure what he meant by that, but the bitterness in his tone was clear.

"I'm sorry that people hunt you," she said. "And I'm glad I was there tonight to help."

He was quiet for a few moments, then he said, "Me, too."

He tightened his embrace, almost as though he was

willing his heat into her. Maybe he was, because her shivering stopped. She wiggled her toes and found that the feeling was returning to them.

"I've read stories about the White Stag," she said. "But never a magical flying polar bear."

He snorted. "You'd know him as the Krampus."

Krampus… She'd heard that name before. It was a Christmas legend about a monster who took away naughty children and ate them. Her stomach felt like it flooded with ice and her skin prickled.

"Krampus is real?" she said, gasping.

"Yeah."

"Oh my God. That is terrifying. Does he actually eat children?"

"What? No." The disgust in his tone was reassuring, until he went on. "He takes them to the Yuletide Kingdom to become servants to the Winter Queen."

"That's not much better."

"As someone who nearly got their head ripped off by the Krampus today, I can tell you that it is decidedly better."

She couldn't argue that point. "Why is he after you? Did he want a wish?"

Again, the deer-guy tensed. It was easy to tell when it happened, with how close he was holding her. This time, he sucked in a breath, too.

"They always do," he said softly.

"I'm sorry." She reached up and clasped the arm that was bent under her head. "That's no way to live."

"It's the only thing I've known for… eternity. I can't remember a time when it was different. Except for tonight."

"Because you turned into a man?"

"Because you gave your wish to me. No one has ever done that before."

"I wasn't thinking," she began.

"You were. I was confused at first, but I sensed the wishes brewing in you. When it came time to put your heart into it, all you wanted was to help me." He nuzzled the back of her head, then pressed his forehead to it. "Thank you."

Her cheeks heated. She had considered other wishes, but how could she not wish to help a living being who was in as much distress as he'd been?

"I still don't know what to call you," she said, eager to change the subject.

"Anything you want." After a brief pause, he said, "Except Buck."

Laughter bubbled up in her chest and spilled out. She was too tired and cold to stop it. Besides, she didn't want to. He joined in with her, and something tightly coiled unwound in her chest. The sound made her feel lighter than she'd felt in months. She rolled onto her back so that she could look at him, which… was a mistake.

He was so beautiful. His dark stubble made his straight teeth gleam whiter in contrast. The skin at the corners of his eyes crinkled when he laughed, their amber depths glowing with a soft golden light. She wanted to reach up and trace his cheekbones, his brow, his jaw. She wanted to… to kiss him.

Being held in his arms made her feel safe for the first time in so long. Maybe forever. She swallowed hard, reaching for a better topic to distract herself from his closeness and warmth. The stories she had read about the White Stag were in a book on Irish folklore. Something Irish, maybe.

"What about Aidan?" she said.

A crease appeared in between his dark eyebrows. "What about him?"

She scowled, then said, "For a name."

He laughed, grinning sheepishly. "Yeah, I figured. Aidan sounds good. May I call you Sylvia?"

"That's my name." She let out a little snort and rolled her eyes.

Smooth. Real smooth.

"It's a beautiful name." His smile softened as he looked down at her. "And it's nice to meet you, Sylvia."

Her heart started to pound at the sound of her name in his low, rumbling voice. Heat built deep in her belly, chasing away the last of her chill. She stared up into his golden eyes and wondered just what she had gotten herself into.

Chapter Four

"So, the Krampus, huh?" Sylvia said. "How worried do I need to be that he's going to show up and wreck the cabin and finish us both off?"

Aidan didn't know how to answer that. He didn't want to frighten her, but he didn't want to mislead her, either. He sighed and shook his head.

"I'm not sure," he said.

"Okay, I'll just add that to my list of worries."

"You have a list of worries?"

"Doesn't everyone?"

"I suppose mortals do," he said.

She snorted. "And immortals have nothing to worry about?"

"Until today, the only thing I worried about was the kinds of wishes people would try to get me to grant."

A small crease appeared between her eyebrows. He wanted to run his thumb over it gently and ease it away.

"I don't understand," she said. "You can't control what people wish for."

"True…" He looked off to the side and half-shrugged.

When he gazed back at her, he knew he had a wicked grin. "But I can usually twist the outcome."

"What do you mean?"

She scooted closer to him, her body pressing tight against his and causing an oddly pleasant sensation to sweep over his skin. It took him a moment to remember what they'd been talking about. He shook his head, as if that might clear it.

Right. Wishes.

"I try to pay attention to what's happening in the mortal realm," he said, "both in nature and among people, so that I can minimize any damage wishes might cause. Like, there might be someone who wishes for riches—that's a really popular one—but I can see in their heart that they would use their wealth to dominate people and cause grief and hardship to others."

"You can see what's in their hearts?"

He shrugged again. "Yeah. It's part of who I am."

She looked pensive for a moment, then said, "What would you do in that case?"

"I'd give them what they want, but I would make sure they regretted it."

"How?"

"People aren't usually very specific with their wishes." He smirked and said, "I once gave a guy five million dollars. He didn't bother asking where it was from."

The corner of her lip quirked up. "And where was it

from?"

"A bank vault," he said. "The police were very grateful for the anonymous tip they received about the location of the stolen money. Which was not easy to manage, what with me being a deer and all."

"That is fantastic."

She laughed and shifted next to him again, bringing their legs closer. Her feet were like ice and he gasped.

She flinched away and said, "Sorry."

"It's okay. You really did freeze out there. Let me help you."

"I don't want to get my cold feet on you." She looked away from him, a deep frown pulling at her lips.

Though his powers were muted, he could still sense the huge spike in emotion within her. It went beyond concern for him or self-consciousness. Someone had tried to break her spirit. The scars of it pulled at his own heart as he sensed the pain in hers.

"Sylvia." He reached to tilt her chin toward him. Her skin was still cold, but softer then he had expected. Defiance burned in her eyes, as if she was prepared to fight him—or she thought he was going to try to start a fight with her.

He kept his voice gentle, and said, "I'm fine now, thanks to you. But you're *not* fine, because you helped me. I'm not okay with that. Please, let me help you."

Her lips parted for a few moments, then she pressed

them together tightly. She turned away, as he expected, but then she scooted back so that her body was pressed against his chest, her legs flush against his. He wrapped his arms around her, pulling the blankets more tightly to entrap the heat. He even brought his mouth beneath the covers for a few breaths, giving her as much of his warmth as he could. She sort of shimmied in his grasp when he did so, a tremor running through her.

"Are you okay?" he asked.

"Yeah, I'm fine." Her voice had reverted to the crisp, efficient tone that she'd used when she first found him—after he'd turned into a man. She had been gentler when she thought she was dealing with an animal and not a magical, immortal being.

"What do I need to know about the Krampus?" she said. "How do I fight him if he comes back for you?"

His heart gave a tug. She still wanted to protect him, even against the Krampus. Most people would run in terror if they saw Krampus in his polar bear form. Aidan had a feeling that Sylvia would stay at his side. She was not 'most people.' He pulled her closer, tangling his feet with hers to try to warm them.

"Aidan?" She looked back at him over her shoulder. "I'm not afraid. Tell me what to do, and I'll fight him."

"I believe you." Aidan lowered his head. "That's what scares *me*."

"Death is nothing to be afraid of," she said. "Living a

half-life is worse. Living a lie." Her eyes pinched at the corners as she spoke. She turned back to face the fire.

This woman…

Aidan's heart did another leap in his chest as his admiration for her grew. He had felt something similar in his deer form a few times when observing people, but this was deeper. The feeling reverberated throughout his entire body, as if his very soul was reaching for her, wanting to pull her closer however it could. He tightened his arms around her ever so slightly. Her body might be cold, but her heart was filled with so much warmth, it flooded through him, granting him an energy he'd never experienced before.

"The Krampus," she prompted, bringing him back to their conversation.

Aidan let out a sigh. "I'm honestly not sure what to tell you. He's always been focused and efficient. He runs several corporations in the mortal realm."

"Seriously?" she said.

"Yes. And then there are his holdings in the Yuletide Kingdom. He's known as Snow there, since that's his dominion."

She glanced at the dark window. Snow had stuck to the glass in thick clumps, illuminated by the fire and the Christmas lights. A thick coating of frost obscured their view of the night sky.

"Any chance this is his doing?" she asked.

"It's very likely. He was probably trying to bury me in snow, then hunt me down at his leisure."

"That's a dick move." She sucked in a small breath, her body stiffening, then said, "Sorry."

Aidan laughed. "Why? It is a dick move."

After a few moments, she relaxed against him again.

"He might succeed in burying you," she said. "Just in the cabin instead of the woods."

"Yes, but when he goes hunting for the White Stag, he'll find nothing."

"Because you're a guy now."

He laughed again. Sylvia had a way of making him laugh. He wished he could do the same for her more often.

"Yes, thanks to you," he said.

"Can you change back? I don't want to think I've trapped you."

His stomach tightened. He had been so intent on getting away from the Krampus, Aidan hadn't really considered how he would change back. There were members of other Faerie Courts he could approach or mortal witches and wizards, but they would all want some form of payment. With his abilities as the White Stag, he could grant them power beyond anything they should have access to. Lying here with Sylvia, basking in the warmth of her body, heart, and mind, he wondered for a moment if he even wanted to turn back.

Sylvia was still waiting for an answer. He could tell by

the way her muscles tensed in his arms. She was ready to act, ready to help. Her heart sang of that so clearly. It was as if her very nature was to help others. His own heart warmed as it basked in the beauty of her soul.

"We'll figure something out." Without thinking, he nuzzled the back of her head once more. She stiffened a bit, her heart thumping against his chest where she was pressed against him. More of that pleasant sensation swept over him.

"So, a guy who can transform into a flying polar bear and has the power to bury us in snow might come knocking on our door any moment," she said. "I'm guessing my shotgun won't have any effect on him."

"The iron pellets will hurt him, but not enough to slow him down. It'll just make him mad."

"I wonder what he wants from you anyway," Sylvia said. "If he's already so powerful and well off, what more could he need?"

Aidan shivered and pulled her closer against his chest. "I sensed the core of his wish when he was chasing me. He wants me to destroy something." It was becoming clearer the longer he was away from their battle as he had time to reflect back on what he had felt.

She tightened her grip on his arm, pressing her body tighter against his instinctively. "What does he want you to destroy?"

"Love." Aidan's own heart ached at the thought.

She tensed, and half-turned in his arms. "What, like all love?"

"No, he's focused on just one loving heart. But any diminishing of love is horrible. At least, to me. The world needs more of it, not less. I can't be part of that."

Her eyes softened and her lips parted. They looked so warm. For a brief moment, he sensed her heart open in invitation. His own leapt in his chest in response. He started to lean closer just as she turned back toward the fire, her expression shuttering.

"You're a good man," she murmured. "Deer. Entity."

Aidan chuckled, pulling her closer again. He thought back over his fight with the Krampus. There was no way Aidan could ever defeat the Krampus in battle, but the way he had fought didn't seem right. Aidan would have expected the Krampus to tackle him or wrestle him to the ground. He'd never expected to have his blood spilled. His shoulder still stung where the Krampus's claws had torn through his flesh before Aidan could turn and take flight.

Take flight…

The Krampus shouldn't have been able to fly after the White Stag. His powers only affected snow. Aidan thought back over his own flight, replaying the moments he had dared to glance behind himself at the raging polar bear chasing him down. There had been snow swirling around him, but not enough to carry him through the sky. That was a power carried by a different Fairy Lord.

What was going on?

Chapter Five

"What is it?" Sylvia asked. Aidan had tensed around her. It was hard not to notice, since he had pretty much enveloped her with his body.

She was definitely heating up in many ways. It had been a long time since anyone had held her close. Honestly, she'd never been held like this. She could practically feel Aidan's desire to bring her comfort and... keep her safe? That was new. She had always felt like she was on her own in that regard. Having someone to watch her back, to focus on her happiness as well as their own—

That was not something she should let herself think about. She sure as heck shouldn't let herself rely on anyone. They always let her down. At least, all the mortals she knew. Maybe Aidan was different.

The stories she'd read portrayed fairies as flakey and mischievous. If anything, they should be even less reliable than humans. Aidan didn't seem like any of the fairy tales she'd read, though. Especially feeling his rock hard body behind her.

Well, not all of it's hard.

The disappointment she felt at that stunned her. Did she actually hope something would happen between them? Her cheeks prickled. She should *definitely* not be entertaining thoughts about *that*. What she should be doing was gathering more information about the magical flying polar bear that might be after her house guest.

"Aidan?" she said, realizing that he hadn't spoken in a bit.

"I was just thinking."

"And I am just asking you to share your thoughts with me." She sucked in a breath, waiting for his response. David wouldn't have appreciated that tone. He would have punished her with emotional distancing or cutting comments. Aidan pulled her closer, resting his chin on the top of her head. Goosebumps swept over her at the tenderness of the gesture.

"The Krampus is one of the two main Fairy Lords in the Court of the Yuletide Fae," Aidan said. "The Winter Queen made him the Lord of Endless Snow. That's where he gets his snow powers."

"Who's the other Lord?"

"The Lord of the North Wind."

She shivered. "It's a good thing you didn't go up against him or we really would have frozen."

"Yeah," Aidan said, his voice pensive.

"What is it?"

"I just… Something isn't right. The Krampus can't fly.

Not like he did while chasing me. That's a power of the North Wind."

"If their powers can be given to them, can they be taken away? Like maybe he took the Lord of the North Wind's power?"

She couldn't believe she was seriously talking about this. It all sounded so crazy. What was even crazier to her was that Aidan was actually listening. She had forgotten what it was like to be taken seriously.

"I can't imagine the Krampus doing that," Aidan said. "He and Lord North are close. Like brothers."

She snorted. "Do they hang out at the North Pole with the Yule Cat?"

"Lord North *is* the Yule Cat. Just like Lord Snow is the Krampus."

Her brain kind of stopped at that for a moment. The Yule Cat was real. The Yule Cat. How was that so hard for her to believe when she was being held in the White Stag's arms?

"The Winter Queen must really like animals," Sylvia said.

"They're shifters. They can appear as humans or in their animal forms at will."

That… put a different spin on things.

"But you can't?" she asked, looking over her shoulder at him.

"No. It took your wish to turn me human. I've never

had this form before, although I've always been curious about it."

"What do you think so far?"

He angled his head from side to side as if thinking, then smiled at her. "I think I like it. Especially this part." He tightened his arms around her. "I've never been able to hold anyone. It's nice. Really nice."

A few choking noises escaped her throat when she tried to respond. Her cheeks heated and goosebumps erupted all over her skin. 'Nice' did not begin to describe what it was like for her to be held in his arms.

"Glad you're enjoying it," she managed at last. That smile of his had her melting. Everything about him did. "When I turned you into a person, did I change who you are?"

"Well, I was always a person. I just used to also be a deer," he said. "But no, this is who I am. Why do you ask?"

Her stomach clenched. What could she say to cover her impulsive question?

Because you're the kindness, gentlest, most tender man I've ever met and that *is why you don't seem possible, not the whole 'being the White Stag' thing.*

"I'm just trying to get everything straight," she said. It wasn't a lie. Not really. She needed to understand what she was dealing with. "So, the Yule Cat, the White Stag, and the Krampus are all real?"

"Yup," he said.

"What about Bigfoot?"

"I've met a couple in my day," he said.

She scoffed a bit at how nonchalant he sounded. They were mostly talking about beings related to Christmas, so she asked about the most obvious name that came to mind.

"Santa?" she said.

"Of course," he replied.

Her heart beat faster. "Really? Santa is real?"

"Yeah."

"What about Rudolph?"

"Him, too."

"I've always loved Rudolph," she murmured.

He tightened his embrace ever so slightly and leaned close to her ear. "Do I need to be jealous?"

"What? No. I mean—"

"Relax, I was only joking." He laughed, his breath fanning across her neck and sending shivers down her spine. "You're taking this all so seriously."

"I don't want to make any mistakes," she asked, only a slight defensive cast to her tone.

"Everyone makes mistakes," he said.

She scoffed again, an odd awkwardness rising in her. "'I'm only human,' right?"

"*Everyone*, makes mistakes," he repeated. "There are wishes that I've granted that… I wish I had tried harder to stop them."

She couldn't believe that he was admitting such thing. The regret in his voice tugged at her heart. She reached up and squeezed his arm.

"You're doing everything you can," she said. "It's on them, what they wished for. You were bound to grant it."

He was silent for a while, then she felt him press his forehead to the back of her hair.

"Thank you," he said.

She squeezed his arm reassuringly, then let out a huge yawn, unable to stifle it. The weariness she felt went bone deep, her muscles felt rubbery, almost as if they'd already fallen asleep without waiting for her brain.

"Sorry," she said, once she could close her jaw again.

"Don't be. You must be exhausted after dragging me all the way here."

"Yeah, you, too, after fighting a flying, magical polar bear." She chuckled and rolled her eyes. "There's something I never thought I'd say."

He joined her light laughter and a feeling of weightlessness suffused her body. She realized that she didn't have to explain herself to this man. Or worry that he would take offense at her reactions in ways she couldn't understand or predict. He was so different from David. Whatever else Aidan was, she was certain that he was kind.

I've been wrong before…

The past year on her own had helped her reconnect

with strengths she had forgotten she'd had. She drew on that to push the doubts aside. She'd always had a gut instinct about people in the past. When she ignored it, that's when things turned out badly, like the years she'd lost to her initially way-too-charming ex-husband. Right now, every fiber of her being was telling her that Aidan was a decent person. Even if he'd recently been a deer.

"I'm actually more relaxed than I've ever been in my existence," he said. "For the first time, no one is hunting me. I have no wishes to grant. Nothing to offer."

"Don't say that." She spoke with more emphasis than she thought she could muster, considering how tired she was. "Just because you can't grant wishes, that doesn't mean you have nothing to offer."

She felt his quick intake of breath and how his chest tightened as he held it, but then he relaxed and pulled her closer. Her eyelids were feeling heavier and heavier. The warmth of the fire in front of her and Aidan's warmth at her back, plus the heaviness of the many blankets and quilts piled on her was lulling her to sleep. She didn't want to sleep, though. She wanted to learn more about this amazing person and the magical world he lived in. Now that she was thinking about it, that was the same world that *she* lived in. She wanted to know everything.

"I don't understand how all these magical beings can be real and nobody knows about it," she said around another huge yawn. Every blink seemed to last longer.

"But people *do* know. That's where the stories come from."

"I suppose. Would you tell me one?" She didn't know where the request had come from and felt a little silly asking. "I mean, if you don't mind."

He laughed again and nuzzled her hair. She let out a contented sort of cooing sound. If she hadn't been so tired, she would have been mortified.

"I don't mind at all," Aidan said. "Let's see…"

He started to speak, his deep, smooth voice lulling her to sleep before he'd made it past, "Once upon a time…"

Chapter Six

"Just because you can't grant wishes, that doesn't mean you have nothing to offer."

Sylvia's words replayed in Aidan's mind over and over. Each time he remembered them, how forcefully she had spoken, his chest filled with warmth that grew stronger. No one had ever valued him for anything aside from his wishes. No one had ever treated him as a friend.

Now, Sylvia was asleep in his arms. How could she be so trusting of him already when they'd just met? He knew he could trust her because he could read her heart. She had no such powers to use with him. He supposed it could be instinct. Still, the fact that she trusted him enough to be so vulnerable with him was humbling. Such trust was nonexistent among the Fae.

She also had courage. It wasn't just shown in how she had leapt in to help him without hesitation. Several times during their conversation, old wounds had threatened to reopen within her. Hurts from an unknown source, but he suspected were tied in with an early love. Those emotional wounds could take the longest to heal, and trust was something that often returned last.

It seemed she had regained the ability to trust herself, and that was the most important thing of all. He knew he didn't have to worry about her in that regard. He *was* worried about whether he was putting her in danger by being with her, though. If the Krampus found him, he could destroy the cabin easily, especially if he lost his temper upon finding Aidan in a form that was useless to him. Even if Sylvia wasn't harmed in that scenario, she'd be left to the elements. Aidan had seen firsthand how dangerous that could be for humans. Now, he had experienced it.

He was human. It was so hard to believe. He had watched people from outside their windows, hidden with magic or darkness and snow, and wondered what it was like to be one of them. To have people to love and who loved him. To be among family.

Sylvia hadn't just been granted her wish in helping him. She had also granted Aidan's. He wanted to enjoy every moment of it and experience everything he could. Eventually, the Krampus would find him, especially if he had somehow gained the power of the Lord of the North Wind. Then, this peaceful dream would be over.

Aidan couldn't fathom how Lord Snow could have taken Lord North's power. The Lord of Endless Snow and the Lord of the North Wind were friends. As close as brothers—the Krampus and the Yule Cat, both servants of the Winter Queen, ruler of the Yuletide Kingdom. Aidan couldn't imagine a situation that would make one of them turn on the other. He knew that North, as the Lord of the North Wind was called among the Fae, had been exiled to the mortal realm, but that was supposed to be temporary. After what Aidan had seen yesterday, he had his doubts. The memory returned to his mind, as clearly as if he was living it again.

A trail of joy led him to the Yuletide Bakery. Lord Kringle, the only Fairy Lord of the Yuletide Kingdom who answered only to himself, had passed this way. The White Stag followed, knowing the pair were kindred spirits. Kringle was one of the few beings in existence whose heart was filled with wishes for others.

The sun hadn't quite risen on the day after Christmas. The White Stag approached the large plate glass window at the front of the bakery. The glass was fogged from the warmth within, a thick coating of frost on the outside. He could still see inside. The snow was falling thickly around him, hiding him from sight. North was inside with a human woman with dark hair and eyes clear as blue crystal. Their smiles and laughter drew the White Stag closer.

So much joy…

Joy and love radiated from the couple as North wrapped his arms around the woman's waist. She was holding a silver tray piled high with cookies that she had been placing in one of the display cases. She turned to North to playfully scold him, but he caught her lips in a kiss.

What must it be like to kiss another? To have arms to hold them close?

The White Stag's wish had begun to form in that moment. He had been curious before, but a yearning sparked in his heart. He wanted to know, to experience that particular joy for himself. If he ever were to be granted a wish of his own, he wanted to experience love. To find the person he was meant to be with.

The wind picked up, biting and harsh against his flank. He stepped back from the window to see Lord Snow emerge from a whirlwind of flakes. His dark suit stretched across his massive shoulders and chest, untouched by the storm. A white silk scarf hung around his neck and he clasped his hands in front of his body, his stance poised with deceptive ease.

"Good evening," Lord Snow said. "I need a word."

The White Stag turned to flee, leaping into the air, but a driving gust of wind knocked him back to the ground. He pranced in a circle, eyes wild with panic at being caged. His panic subsided as he measured his foe—the one he was sure was hunting him in that moment. The heart within Lord Snow raged with grief and confusion.

"I need you to help my friend," Lord Snow said.

He turned to the window and looked within, his lips

turning down in a frown as he stared at the happy couple. A creeping cold filled Lord Snow's heart. In that moment, he was the Krampus, the monster mortals feared. The White Stag knew what his wish would be. He wanted to destroy the love between North and the woman inside.

The Stag couldn't allow it. He turned to flee, leaping into the air once more. Again, the wind knocked him to the ground with bruising force. Lord Snow stepped closer.

"I don't want to hurt you," he said. "This is just business. The Yuletide Kingdom needs both Fairy Lords. I can't keep things going forever on my own. North needs to come home."

A longing swept through the Krampus. Aching loneliness and loss that again gave the White Stag pause. He couldn't let the Krampus destroy a love that shined as brightly as that between North and his mate. If the Stag couldn't flee, he would fight. He scraped a hoof against the cobblestone street in warning. The Krampus stared at his hoof and smirked.

"If that's how it's going to be, okay," he said. "We do this the hard way."

Brilliant light enveloped him, so bright it burned the White Stag's eyes. The Krampus's form grew and morphed, turning into an enormous, monstrous polar bear. His teeth were so huge, they didn't entirely fit in his mouth, his claws stretched unnaturally far from his paws, and his pelt was filled with sparkling motes of energy. The door to the bakery opened and Lord North stepped outside.

"Snow?" he said. "What the heck is going on out here?"

The Krampus turned to his friend, and in that moment of distraction, the Stag knew he must flee. He turned and ran as rapidly as he could toward the edge of town, far from humans who might be injured if the Krampus lost his temper. He leapt into the air, at last able to take flight, heading toward the forest outside of town.

The night sky was not the refuge it had always been as the Krampus gave chase in a hunt that lasted days. Another gust of wind caught the White Stag, sending him tumbling. Snow whipped into his eyes, blinding him. He could sense the Krampus nearby with his heart hardened with destructive purpose. The Stag lashed out with his antlers, connecting with a pelt as hard as ice. The arms of the bear's form reached for the Stag, but he kicked away. Just then, the wind picked up further, spinning both out of control.

Pain burned across his shoulders as the Krampus's claws raked across his shoulder. They tumbled apart, the snow and wind swallowing each of them up. Panic tore at the White Stag's mind. He pushed all of his power into his escape. If he couldn't experience love himself, he could at least protect it.

A wave of warmth enveloped him, almost calling to him. He followed it deeper into the woods, latching onto it like a beacon. As his strength failed him, he crashed through the trees, their heavy branches tangling in his antlers and dragging him further toward the ground. The frozen earth stunned him as he struck it, even with the padding of snow from the surrounding storm. Exhaustion won out over his panic for a moment, and in that moment, he felt a strange peace. He knew that someone was coming to help him. He wasn't sure how, but he was certain of it.

And then Sylvia had arrived.

Aidan looked down at the woman sleeping in his arms, the same peace he had felt radiating from her. The emotional wounds she carried should make her not trust him, but her heart told her she could do so. Just as his heart was speaking to him now, telling him… something he didn't understand quite yet, but that he would strive to figure out with her help. He knew she would keep helping him. It was her nature to help others, just as it was his.

He pulled the blankets closer around her, making sure she would stay warm, and focused on memorizing every detail of the experience. He didn't want to forget anything about this moment. Or about her.

Chapter Seven

Sylvia had been buried alive. At least, that's what it felt like, waking up under so many blankets. She must have fallen asleep in front of the fire, as she had planned. As she shifted beneath the weight of them, she realized she was in her underwear. The events of the evening before came crashing back into her mind, making her heart race. She craned her neck over her shoulder, but found that she was alone. Had it been a dream? But then, why was she in her underwear?

Tentatively, she said, "Aidan?"

"One sec," he called back from the bathroom.

Her eyes widened. It hadn't been a dream. The deer-man she had found in the woods was real and he was still here. And she was mostly naked. She shimmied out from under the covers, the cold air hitting her like diving into icy waters. She threw more logs on the glowing embers of the fire and stirred them up with the poker quickly, then bolted up the stairs, ignoring the goosebumps rocketing over her skin and the way her muscles tensed from the cold of the cabin.

In the loft, she grabbed a fresh outfit. She quickly tore off what she was wearing and put on fresh underwear, then a set of thermal underwear, thick sweats, and two pairs of socks. She ran her fingers through her hair, though she couldn't imagine what prompted her to do so, then turned around and screamed. Aidan was standing at the top of the stairs, a huge smile on his face.

"How long have you been standing there?" she demanded.

"Not long." He pointed at the staircase that hugged one of the walls. "That was fun. I'm figuring things out." He marched in place as he turned back to her, his smile somehow growing even broader.

Her eyebrows hitched up her forehead as the movement drew her attention to his muscled thighs dusted with just the right amount of hair and, more enthralling, the quite impressive package that dangled between them. She hadn't really gotten a good look the day before and shouldn't be looking now. She forced her gaze up, trying to hurry, but her eyes would not be rushed.

The strong arms that had wrapped around her all night were larger than she'd thought, but not too bulky. He had a narrow waist, perfect rows of abs, and a sculpted chest covered in a fine coat of dark hair that was absolutely mesmerizing. It trailed down his abdomen, bringing her focus right back to his groin.

"It's not as hard as I thought it would be," he said.

"Hmm?" she said, then remembered that his eyes were 'up there.' She finally managed to meet his gaze, though she could feel that her own eyes were round as saucers.

"Walking on two legs," he said. "Human stuff. Although, I think I could use some clothes. My muscles are starting to get kind of shaky and I think my teeth are getting ready to chatter again.

"Oh gosh, I'm so sorry," she said. She ran to the closet and pulled out one of the plastic storage bins that she'd been meaning to go through. "I think I have some old clothes of my ex's around here."

"Your ex?"

"Yeah." She hesitated, but then said, "My ex-husband."

Thankfully, Aidan didn't ask more questions as she dug through the clothes in the bin. She pulled out some sweatshirts and sweatpants, hoping the fabric would stretch enough to fit him. David was tall, but not as filled out as Aidan. She found some thermal underwear and thick wool socks as well. With the whole bundle in her arms she staggered to the bed and dumped them on the mattress.

"Here you go," she said, gesturing toward them. "Oh, you need to start with the thermal underwear, then I'd do the socks, then the sweats."

Aidan nodded toward the pile, approaching the bed. "Thanks."

Sylvia wasn't sure what to do. She didn't feel right gawking at him—at least morally. Physically, watching his muscles move as he walked and picked up the clothing was pure poetry. His backside was so taut, it made something deep inside her coil in response. She quickly turned around, settling on that as a compromise. He might need her if he had questions, so she shouldn't go too far away.

"These are great," he said. "Really warm. I can see why humans wear things like them. I don't think I need the thermal garments, though."

"You might regret that later," she said, glancing back over her shoulder. His sweatpants were already on. The muscles of his back rippled as he pulled the sweatshirt over his head. "The cabin gets really cold..."

He turned back to her and she started guiltily. She wanted to turn around again, but the smile he cast at her was so warm, she couldn't bring herself to look away from it.

"If I get cold, we can always crawl under the blankets again, right?" he asked. "You would probably be cold, too, if it came to that."

She felt her eyes widen as she nodded her head like an idiot. "Yeah. Good point." She bet certain other parts of his anatomy would make a very good point.

What had gotten into her? She pinched her eyes shut and shook her head, willing away any other tawdry thoughts that might pop into her mind.

"You okay?" he asked.

"Yes, sure." She opened her eyes again, nodding vigorously. "You?"

"I think I'm hungry." He rubbed his stomach. "Do you have any ideas about what I should eat?"

"I um… I have some Christmas cookies left over that we can snack on till I can cook something. I got them from this great place called the Yuletide Bakery."

His eyebrows lifted. "I know that place."

"Really?" That seemed like too much of a coincidence.

"Yeah." He sat on the bed and pulled on the thick socks. His eyebrows rose and he wiggled his feet, staring at them. "Oh wow. That is an experience."

"What is?"

"My toes were freezing before. These socks are so warm and soft. They feel like they're giving my feet hugs."

She burst out laughing, then pinched her lips shut.

"What?" he said.

"Nothing." She was having trouble not laughing more. He was just so earnest and sweet. He gave her a look, and she shrugged. "I've just never seen someone so happy about a pair of socks."

He stood and crossed the room to stand close to her. As he approached, her breath caught in her chest. She wasn't nervous, she was excited. It had been so long since she'd felt anything like that. He stopped so close that she could lean forward and kiss him if she wanted to. Not that she wanted to.

Of course I want to.

"Well, they *are* my first pair of socks," he said.

Right. Because he had been a deer recently. She kept forgetting.

"How are you so good at being human?" she blurted out.

His eyes widened and his lips parted as if her question surprised him. She was stammering incoherently, trying to form an apology when his soft smile took her breath away yet again. He laughed and shook his head.

"You spend enough time on the outside looking in, you pick up a few things," he said. "I've had a long time to wonder what it's like to be human, but I never had a chance to actually try it out till I met you."

"I'm glad you're enjoying it," she said, and meant it. If he was trapped in human form because of her and didn't want to be, she would feel awful. He didn't seem upset at all, though. He seemed… happy. Sylvia resolved to help him enjoy being human as much as she could. "Let's get you those cookies."

His smile brightened and she couldn't help smiling back. She went first down the stairs, angling her head over her shoulder as much as was safe to watch that he didn't trip. Even if he did, there wasn't much she could do for him except cushion his fall. Which wouldn't exactly be a hardship. She imagined him landing on top of her, their faces close, breath mingling…

I have got to get a hold of this.

Back on the main floor, she hurried to the fridge, grateful that the solar panels had remained clear enough of snow to keep working. She grabbed a couple of mugs and filled them with milk, then set the mugs and box of cookies on the little island that separated the kitchen from the great room. Aidan sat on one of the stools next to the granite countertop, watching everything she did with interest. She circled around to sit next to him, then opened the box.

"Dig in," she said.

"Thanks." He picked up a Chocolate Crinkle Cookie and took a bite. His eyes rolled shut and he groaned.

Sylvia barely managed to suppress a similar sound. Watching his jaw work, even his throat as he swallowed… She wanted to say her reaction to Aidan was just a matter of how long she'd been alone, but she knew it was more than that. He was the most gorgeous man she'd ever seen. Thank goodness he wasn't attracted to her. There was no way she'd be able to resist him. Yes indeed, she sure was glad that he had just been a deer recently and couldn't possibly be attracted to her. Very glad. Not at all disappointed.

Chapter Eight

Sylvia had the oddest expression on her face. It was shielded—or at least, as shielded as she could manage—but her heart was singing loud and clear, broadcasting her longing. Aidan wasn't sure what it was she wanted. If he could figure it out, he would give it to her. It was the least he could do for her after she'd made his own wish come true.

Being a human was amazing. He loved having arms. And hands! He reached out to pick up another cookie, smiling at how his fingers responded to his desires. And the cookies… The one he had eaten had melted in his mouth, a burst of flavor coating his tongue and flooding his senses as he ate it. No wonder humans were always talking about how much they loved chocolate.

"These are amazing," he said.

"Have another." She scooted the box closer, taking a Crinkle Cookie for herself.

He ate another, then another, taking his time and savoring the flavors. The box was filled with an assortment that were as pleasing to look at as to eat. Small round cookies, flat ones decorated like snowmen, orangish-brown cookies that smelled of cinnamon. He relished each one, trying all the different flavors. Sylvia had only eaten a couple. He looked over to see her staring at him, her eyes wide and lips slightly parted. A sharp spike of guilt surged through her and she looked away.

"Am I eating too many?" Aidan asked.

"No, not at all. You're just… really enjoying them." She glanced at him, then quickly picked up another cookie and held it close to her mouth. "You said you know of the Yuletide Bakery. How is that?"

"It's run by the Yule Cat."

Sylvia had just started on the cookie. Her eyes widened at his words and she made an odd noise that turned into coughing. Aidan sat up straighter, unsure of what to do. She waved him off, then picked up her mug and gulped down most of its contents. Finally, she set it down and cleared her throat.

"The Yule Cat?" she said.

"Yeah. Lord of the North Wind." Although, he wasn't too sure about that second part anymore. "He's living with a human woman that he fell in love with, but I think he's still doing most of the baking."

"A human woman? Really?" That longing flared up in her again for a moment, but it quickly disappeared beneath a beautiful playfulness. Sylvia narrowed her eyes, picking up another cookie and holding it up. "So, you're telling me that a Fairy Lord made this cookie?"

Aidan nodded.

She picked up another cookie. "And this one?"

He laughed, then started pointing at cookies as he said, "And this one. And that one, too. Why is it so hard to believe?"

"I don't know. You think of a Fairy Lord, you don't imagine them baking for humans." Her eyes widened and she stiffened on her stool. "Unless these are magic and meant to cast a spell on people."

Aidan laughed again, shaking his head. "Nothing like that. Except for the magic of chocolate."

He picked up another Crinkle Cookie and brought it to his nose, closing his eyes as he took a deep breath and enjoyed the scent of it. When he opened his eyes, Sylvia was staring at him again.

"What?" he asked.

"Nothing." She shook her head, her eyes widening as she looked away.

Every time she did that gesture, her heart sort of trembled and shuttered. He could sense a wound there. One that had been healing, but still left a mark. Reaching out, he covered her hand with his. Again, her eyes widened as she stared at their hands resting on the counter, but her heart unfurled, the longing he sensed from her flowing into him like a warm breeze.

"You can speak freely with me," Aidan said. "I like

hearing your thoughts."

She half-smiled, but it was a rueful look. Worse, she pulled her hand away, holding them both on her lap and shaking her head. He wanted to encourage her, but knew too well what it was like to feel pursued. Instead, he sat with her silently, giving her the time and space she needed to decide what she was ready to share. After a few minutes of silence, she glanced at him quickly, then around the room, that oddly muted smile still in place.

"It's weird," she said.

He waited a few moments before saying, "What is?"

"The way I feel with you." She shook her head and laughed. "Almost… safe."

He reached for her hands again, slowly lifting them from her lap to rest on his knees. Warmth flowed through his arms and chest, then down through his abdomen. His skin tingled where they touched, his heart was beating faster, especially when he realized she wasn't pulling away again.

"I have been hunted constantly for as long as I can remember," he said. "And I can remember a very, very long time. It's hard to feel safe after that."

She nodded. "I can imagine."

He smiled at her and said, "I feel safe with you, too."

Her eyes widened. "How? I mean, you just met me."

"I can feel people's hearts," he said. "Kind of like Cupid."

She gasped, then said, "Cupid is real?"

Aidan stared at her for a few moments, one eyebrow arched and a soft tilt to his lips.

"Cupid is real," she said, nodding.

"I felt your heart in the grove where you found me," he said. "Everyone who's hunted me, they did so because they wanted something for themselves. All you wanted was to help *me*."

"I wanted other things at first." She shook her head. "When I remembered the stories about you granting wishes."

"I was aware." He chuckled. "Even then, your heart was open to others. I sensed the goodness in you."

She rolled her eyes and let out a brief laugh. Aidan tightened his grip on her hands.

"You are a good person, Sylvia. At your core, you have the most wonderful heart of anyone I've ever met."

"Hanging out with fairies, I suppose that makes sense," she said. "From the stories I've read, they aren't very nice."

"Don't do that," he said.

That look came to her eyes again. What was it humans called it? 'Like a deer caught in headlights.' He would have chuckled at the irony of it if he wasn't so focused on helping her understand what he saw in her.

"You don't have to diminish yourself for others," he said. "Especially me."

She let out a breath through her nose and laughed awkwardly. After a moment, she said, "Thanks."

Again, she pulled her hands away from his. This time, the absence of her touch echoed in his heart. He had never sensed that hollowness in himself before. An emptiness that longed to be filled.

That longing…

Sylvia picked up another cookie and chuckled. "I can't believe the Yule Cat made these. Does that mean the hot guy who owns the bakery can turn into a cat?"

Aidan's skin prickled and his chest tightened. He felt himself frowning, but wasn't sure why.

"The hot guy?" Aidan asked, unsure of why he was fixating on that.

She shrugged. "Have you *seen* him?"

"Yeah." Aidan didn't want the odd sharpness he felt around the topic to make her withdraw again. At the same time, he needed to sort through his feelings. "I didn't know you were attracted to him," he said, as noncommittally as he could.

"No way." She snorted and shook her head. "I'm not attracted to him at all. The guy is objectively hot, but not my type."

The sharp ache in his chest immediately blunted. "What is your type?"

Again, her eyes widened as she stared at him. Her cheeks turned bright red, the flush spreading down her neck. She crammed a cookie into her mouth and looked away, but not before he'd seen everything he needed—not before he'd sensed that longing inside her blaze to life once more. A longing he understood so much better now that he had felt it himself.

Her heart was reaching out. Reaching toward *him*.

Aidan's chest filled with warmth, his heart fairly bursting with it. His mouth went dry and his hands twitched with the urge to reach for her again. The arms that were so new to him wanted nothing more than to wrap her in his embrace. Something in her called out to him and everything in him responded. His very essence reached for her, and he knew she felt the same. He just had to convince her it was safe for her to reach back.

Chapter Nine

How could she avoid answering Aidan's question without lying? Sylvia didn't want to lie to him, ever. But she also didn't want to admit that he was exactly her type. From his dark hair and strong jaw to his golden-brown eyes and sensual lips. Not to mention his absolutely sculpted body, just the thought of which had her fidgeting on her stool.

But it was more than that. It was his easy smile and his warm laughter. It was how he listened to her and encouraged her to open up. How he didn't make her feel lesser or silly, but valued and… worthy.

She wasn't ready to admit how much she liked him, even to herself. So she dodged the question instead of answering.

"North looks way too much like David," she said.

"David?"

"My dickweed ex-husband. He and I used to come here every year for Christmas. I got the cabin in the divorce, so I'm enjoying it."

Aidan's eyebrows furrowed and he angled his head to

the side. "Dickweed?" he said. "Is that some kind of plant?

She laughed and shook her head. "No, it's a… It's kind of a name we call people we don't like. I probably shouldn't use it, but 'if the shoe fits…'"

The furrow between his eyebrows deepened. God, he had amazing eyes. And face. And everything.

She sighed. "You don't understand any of this, do you?"

He looked off to the side, eyes narrowed as if he was thinking really hard. Then his lips pulled into a grin as he looked back at her. Her stomach started doing happy flips, her skin tingling at the sight of that smile. Then her brain kicked in.

"Wait a minute," she said.

He burst out laughing, then said, "I'm sorry. It was just too hard to resist."

She scowled at him playfully, narrowing her eyes. "So, you're up to date on all our mortal slang?"

"Mortal slang." He made a face as if contemplating the phrase, but nodded. "I guess you could say that."

"More things you've picked up over the years?" she asked.

He laughed and nodded. "Yeah.

He looked down at his body, prompting her to do the same. It was in no way a hardship, as more of that electric awareness zinged through her, lighting her up more and more as she knew him better.

"Two legs is kind of an adjustment," he said. "But the rest of it is pretty fun. There's a bunch of stuff I don't quite get, though."

"Is there anything I can help you with?" She swallowed hard, her mouth going dry. There were so many things she would like to help him with.

"Well, like this stuff."

He pulled up his sweatshirt, revealing those perfect rows of abs, tapered waist, and broad chest. With his free hand, he plucked at the dark hair that lightly coated his pectoral muscles. Sylvia felt like a nuke had gone off in her nethers. Her core fairly throbbed at the sight of him, her belly flooding with heat. Did he have to turn into such a gorgeous human? She was practically drooling as she stared.

"It's completely useless for keeping me warm," he said. "Why is it even there?"

"It's um…" Her fingers curled with the urge to bury themselves in it. How could she explain without humiliating herself? She finally landed on, "It's decorative."

"Decorative." He made his thinky face again, but this time, she figured it was for real. "Like for attracting a mate?" One eyebrow hitched up, as if he couldn't believe the prospect.

"Mm-hmm," she said, her eyes glued to his chest.

"Is it working?" His lips pulled into a lopsided smile—

not quite a smirk, but close enough that she had a feeling he knew how his body was affecting her. Her only response was to narrow her eyes and glare at him.

Aidan looked down at his body again and made a, "Hmph," sound. He plucked at one hair, then winced. "Ouch."

"Don't do that."

She leaned forward to put her hand over his to keep him from hurting himself. Unfortunately—or fortunately —he had already moved his hand away, and she ended up planting hers on his chest. Her fingers curved reflexively, burrowing through the coarse hairs as more heat flooded her. Her cheeks tingled and her nipples tightened, her skin rising in goosebumps.

His eyebrows hitched up his forehead and his mouth dropped open on a quick intake of breath. She tried to move her hand away, but he grabbed it and held it in place. Damn, he was fast. Angling his head to the side, he stared at her with an intensity that made her core thump and her muscles coil. She wanted to jump on him, ride him down to the couch, and show him just what all those new parts were for.

"Now, this is interesting," he said.

She licked her suddenly dry lips. "What is?"

"How this feels," he said, his voice growing low and husky. "Your touch."

"How... How does it feel?"

He took a step closer, his grip still keeping her hand tight to his chest as he let his shirt fall over their hands.

"Good," he said, leaning closer. "Very good."

His warm breath fanned her face, his lips almost brushing hers when she snapped herself out of it and turned away. This wasn't a good idea. He wasn't even human. She had probably lost her mind and was hallucinating the whole thing anyway. But if that last was true, why not go with it and enjoy what her broken mind was offering her?

She had thought she was doing better over the last year. Her confidence was higher and she was even starting to chat with people when she went in to town for supplies or just a bit of being around other humans, even if it was just to sit in a bakery by herself, eating cookies and sipping coffee. A bakery apparently run by someone who wasn't human.

"What is it?" Aidan asked, his voice exceedingly gentle.

"I um…" She shook her head, trying to find an excuse. She had told herself she'd never lie to him, but broke her word as she said, "It's just too fast."

He chuckled and she felt the vibration of his laugh through her hand. His heart beat strong and fast beneath it.

"One thing I never understood about humans was how long it takes them to listen to their hearts," he said. "Your lives are so short, and yet you sometimes waste years waiting for 'the timing to be right'—whatever that means."

"It means things take a certain amount of time."

"The timing is right when you choose for it to be right," he said. "I know you've been hurt before. Betrayed. If you let that close your heart to love, then that is a choice you're making. One that I would never wish on anyone, especially you."

She stared at him, eyes round, feeling paralyzed, like... like a deer in headlights. The thought might have made her laugh if she hadn't sensed how important the next few moments would be for her life. She wanted so much to let herself lean into him, to give in to the desire she felt. But he was talking about a lot more than physical intimacy. With him, she knew it would be all or nothing. That's what he would want and what she would want to give him. Was she really ready for that? To open herself up to that risk?

"Don't think," he said. "Just feel. Tell me what you feel when you look at me."

"Hope." The word sprang out too quickly for her to stop it. She snapped her mouth shut before any other truths could escape from it. Aidan's eyes widened and he smiled.

"I can still feel your heart," he said, gently rubbing the hand he held to his chest, his warmth seeping into her. "Even in this form. It's reaching for me. I know it seems dangerous and scary. That's why they call it 'falling in love.' But my heart is open to yours. It's waiting. Let yourself fall." His voice became even gentler as he said, "I'll catch you."

The room seemed to spin around her as her head grew light. Her heart was pounding, her skin electrified with the awareness of his closeness, her hand beneath his shirt, his skin beneath her palm. This was what she wanted. His heart, even more than his gorgeous body. She wanted his kindness, his warmth, his... love. She wanted to love him. And she knew all she had to do to get her wish was let herself go. She stepped closer, grabbing the back of his neck with her free hand to pull him into a kiss.

•

Chapter Ten

Heat blasted through Aidan's body, stronger than anything he'd ever known. Sylvia was kissing him, her soft lips pressed against his, her body close. He released the hand he had been holding to his chest, but only to clasp her hips and pull her closer. The moment he did, she wrapped both arms around his neck, trapping him against herself. For once, he didn't mind.

She ran her tongue along the seam of his lips, both as an invitation and a plea. He opened to her, deepening the kiss as they explored each other. The taste of sweet ginger and chocolate flooded his senses. She ran her fingers through his hair, her nails lightly scraping along his scalp and sending waves of goosebumps over him.

He slid his arms around her back, holding her even closer. This was so different from last night. That same fullness was in his heart, but this time, it filled his entire body, flooding him with need. His cock stiffened, the soft fabric of his sweatpants was an exquisite torture against the sensitized flesh. He had never felt anything like it.

"Sylvia," he murmured, moving his kisses along her

neck. "Tell me what to do."

"What do you mean?" she said, in a breathless voice.

"I want to be closer to you. But I've never…"

She stiffened against him, taking in a swift breath that she held. For a moment, it felt as though his heart had stopped, fear lacing through him that she would pull away. That was the opposite of what he wanted, but he would deal with it if that was what she needed.

Slowly, she let out her breath, then she kissed his neck, nibbling her way up to his ear. She sucked his earlobe between her teeth, lightly grazing it, and another wave of sensation swept through him.

"Let me show you," she whispered against his ear.

Relief made him almost giddy. He closed his eyes and nodded, leaning his head against hers. She drew her fingers through his hair again, tilting his head and kissing him deeply, till the room seemed to spin. Her hands slid down his chest, then under his shirt, her fingertips playing with his abs.

Electric pleasure cantered along his nerves, lighting up every part of him—especially his cock. It throbbed and ached, pulling more of his attention to it, to her hands lingering so close. She ran the backs of her fingertips along his torso, then down to his waistband, lifting it so she could reach in with her other hand to stroke him as she moved her lips to his neck once more.

He sucked in a breath at the first brush of her cool

fingers against his hot flesh, his muscles trembling with the need for more. She wrapped her hand around him in a firm grip, and pleasure exploded through him. The chill in the air vanished as his body heated beneath her touch. She ran her hand along his shaft in a firm stroke, brushing her thumb over his tip when she reached it.

His knees felt weak, but he locked them in place, intent on experiencing every drop of pleasure she was giving him, memorizing it. Each stroke of her hand made him feel closer to her, his chest filling with warmth. She was bringing this forth from deep within him, reaching into his physical essence to trigger a greater pleasure than he'd ever known. She released her grip, but only to tug his pants down a bit below his waist, freeing his cock.

The air was chilly, but he trusted her to warm him. She shifted away from him, prompting him to finally open his eyes. She dropped to her knees, her focus intent on his cock, swollen lips parted as she took him into her mouth. He gasped, his balance wavering as sensations almost too intense to bear flooded him. His entire body thrummed with pleasure and an even greater need for more.

She gripped his ass, fingers digging into his backside and helping to keep him steady. Instinctively, he reached for her, his own fingers burrowing into her hair, somehow increasing the intimacy of what she was doing. Once he had steadied, she brought one hand back to grip him tightly, stroking his shaft in time with the movement of her lips, sucking him in deeper.

Pressure built in his cock and belly, spreading out through his entire body, along with more of that delicious heat. She swirled her tongue along his flesh, moving her hand and mouth faster, sucking harder. The pressure built till he thought he might burst. In a flash of ecstasy that threatened to bring him to his knees, the pressure exploded through him.

His skin erupted in goosebumps, his blood pounded in his veins. Wave after wave of pleasure crashed through him as he pulsed in her mouth. Sylvia held on, keeping time with his movements, drawing out his pleasure till he thought he might black out.

Finally, she slowed, then released him and pulled his sweats back into place. He looked down at her, his chest heaving with panting breaths. That had been the most amazing experience of his very long existence. And he wanted more. So much more.

Her eyes were wide as she looked up at him, uncertain. Could she actually be doubting that she had done anything but given him an extraordinary gift? He knelt in front of her, cupping her face in his hands as he stared at her in wonder. Then he kissed her, willing all of his passion, all of his hope and longing and dreams for what their future could hold into that kiss. She gripped his wrists, holding on tight as she kissed him back with just as much passion. When they were both breathless, he pulled back, but left their foreheads touching.

"Thank you," he said.

Her cheeks pinked as she said, "You're welcome."

"I would really, really like to make love to you now," he said.

Her eyes widened again, but then she laughed. "I'd like that, too. You might need a minute, though. Human bodies and all that."

He joined her laughter and nodded, envisioning their bodies entwined, the firelight kissing her pale skin. Human bodies, though…

"I'll build up the fire," he said. "And you can maybe help me out with some of those layers."

Her cheeks darkened further, but she nodded. He took her hand and rose, pulling her after him. The idea of not touching her was unwelcome, but he knew he needed both hands to tend the fire. He didn't want anything to get in the way of giving her as much pleasure as she'd just given him. He squeezed her hand before letting go, then turned to the fire and started piling on logs, working them into position till he had a blaze going.

Behind him, the soft sound of fabric sweeping over Sylvia's skin brought more goosebumps to his. Seeing her almost naked last night hadn't had the same meaning. He couldn't wait to see her again, now that he'd experienced the kind of pleasure these forms could give each other. He wanted to explore everything, to bring her to that precipice of ecstasy, then plunge into it together. It was all he wanted, forever.

His wish to experience what it was like to be human had started out as a curiosity. Now that Sylvia was in his life, it was a necessity. He had to be with her. Had to hold her and kiss her and make love with her. His heart seemed to swell as he realized that he truly never wanted to change back. Not if it meant leaving her.

The fire was blazing, putting out almost more heat than he could bear when he rose and turned back to her. She stood in the middle of the pillows, staring at him with wide eyes and a clenched mouth. She held a blanket in front of her—not wrapped around her to keep her warm. It was as though she was trying to hide from him.

The firelight caught in her hair and made it blaze like molten copper. Her soft, heart-shaped face had a dusting of freckles across her nose that made him want to kiss it. She stared at him with large brown eyes that he could gaze into forever.

"What?" she asked, nervously shifting her weight from one foot to the other, as if she was considering taking flight.

The sentiment was so familiar, it brought a brief flutter of pain to his heart. He hated that something in her life had made her feel this way. Insufficient. And yet, he was sure it was part of what had made her so strong, part of who she was. He would never change anything about her.

He shook his head and kept his voice gentle as he said, "You. In all the time I've existed, you're the most beautiful woman I've ever seen."

Chapter Eleven

Sylvia couldn't have heard him right. Aidan had been around for millennia, probably. He'd seen more women than she could conceive of. Maybe they looked different to him when he was in his deer form. The 'activity' they had just finished probably worked in her favor, too, along with what they were about to do. She realized she was staring at him again and looked away with an uneasy laugh.

"You don't have to do that," he said.

"Do what?"

"Hide from me. I will never, through my words or actions, cause you harm. Not if I can help it." He spoke so earnestly, it was impossible not to believe him. "May I see you? Please?"

When he asked like that, how could she say no? Her heart was beating in her throat, butterflies threatening to overflow her stomach, but she at least managed to nod. She took a deep breath, then lowered the blanket and let it drop to the ground.

Aidan was silent and still. She felt her cheeks heat and fought the desperate urge to cover herself with her hands if nothing else. Instead, she forced herself to stay put.

"Sylvia, look at me."

It took her a moment to will her eyes toward him, and her cheeks burned like she had a fever. She didn't want to see his judging gaze. When David had looked at her naked, she had always come up short. Too flat-chested, no butt, yet too many muscles from trying to stay strong enough to lift larger animals at the vet school—and with no fashion sense to cover up her flaws. David could go on and on about her faults, and often did. Now, she was staring at the most unbelievably gorgeous man she'd ever seen, and trying not to catalogue everything that was wrong with her. Everything that would eventually drive him away.

Aidan pulled his shirt over his head and tossed it aside, then quickly did the same with the rest of his clothing.

"Really look at me," he said.

Her breath came more quickly as she eagerly catalogued all of his strengths. His strong, muscled thighs and arms, his broad chest and shoulders, his narrow waist and hips. His skin was lightly tanned, complementing the dark hair that coated his legs and chest. He was already hard again, the sight of his erection sent a pulse of pleasure between her legs.

She had been aching for him since the moment she'd taken him in her mouth. Since before then, actually. It all felt like a dream. There was no way this beautiful man was interested in her. No way that he would have shared that intimacy with her—his first intimacy.

"I do want you," he said, gesturing toward his cock. "And I'm not going anywhere."

Her gaze snapped to his and her lips pressed into a thin line. "Can you read my mind?" she asked.

"No. And even if I could, I wouldn't without your permission." He looked at her chest and said, "But I can see your heart. I can't not see it. Your fear. Your worry." He stepped forward, closing the distance between them, but not touching her. "I don't want anything to happen between us that you don't want, too. But I want us to be together. I look at you, and I see a part of myself that I didn't know I was missing. I see my other half."

"I don't know how you do it." Again, she spoke without meaning to. This time, there was no crushing self-doubt that accompanied it. No fear over how he'd react.

"Do what?" he asked.

"Make me believe. In you. In me. In us. In… love."

His gold-tinged eyes widened and his lips parted. Her heart pounded again, but for a very different reason. She reached for him, pulling herself up to kiss him. The butterflies still filled her belly, but when they overflowed, it sent warmth and awareness through her entire body, like they were fluttering through every cell, filling her with light and love.

Yes, it was happening fast. Yes, it didn't make any sense—for her to be falling in love with the White Stag in human form. But she didn't care. All she cared about was holding Aidan close, being in his arms and feeling his warm lips and his even warmer heart.

He lowered them to the pillows, rolling so that he was on his back and she was straddling him. He gripped her hips, lining up the tip of his shaft against her core. She rose up, hands against his chest and arms straight to give herself better leverage to move.

Ever so slowly, she lowered herself onto him, delighting in the exquisite sensations rippling through her body as he parted her flesh. His fingers dug into her backside, his eyes clenched shut. Pleasure pulsed out from where they were joined, warming her even more than the fire raging in the hearth. When she had taken all of him in, he gasped, pressing her down against him tight.

"Are you okay?" she asked.

He shook his head. "It feels too good. I want to last for you."

"It's okay if you don't," she said. "We can always do it again."

His eyes snapped open, their golden light glowing brightly. He might look like a man, but they were a beautiful reminder that he was still a magical being.

"I don't want you to have to wait," he said. "I want to give you pleasure, like you did for me."

She tilted her head and looked away, her cheeks prickling. How could she feel self-conscious while they were in the middle of this?

"There are plenty of other things we can do," she said.

"Really?" His eyebrows lifted and his grip on her hips relaxed a bit. More than anything, his eagerness to please her was reassuring for her.

"Yes, really."

"What kinds of things?"

She laughed, her heart filling with warmth. She didn't think she had ever laughed while making love before. Aidan was opening her up to all kinds of new experiences. With him at her side, she wasn't afraid of them.

"Let's start with this," she said, then lifted herself up along his shaft.

His head pressed harder against the pillows as he sucked in a breath, his hands firm on her backside as she slid back down to take him in deep. His chest rose and fell sporadically as she moved, like he couldn't catch his breath. She'd never felt more desired before. It was its own kind of pleasure, intoxicating in how it empowered her. She was doing this to him—for him. Because he wanted her. Because he loved her.

Of everything else happening, that was the most unbelievable thing. Yet she believed it. She believed in him.

"Move your hips," she said. "Rise to meet me."

He nodded, rocking his hips against hers in time with her movements. Each millimeter of friction sent waves of heat cascading along her nerves, a core of molten lava building deep in her belly. Before long, he was thrusting faster, landing harder. Her body was on fire as she rode him, her skin prickling with awareness wherever they touched. For the first time, she let herself be lost in the sensations, giving herself over to the pleasure he was giving her, to the ecstasy of their union.

The heat rose higher, a delicious pressure building in her belly. For a moment, time seemed suspended, the precipice he had brought her to loomed before her. Then she plunged over it, her body flooded with heat as pleasure pulsed through her body in wave after wave. Aidan cried out a moment after, his thrusting becoming frenzied, his cock throbbing deep within her. He pressed her tight against him, back still arched and eyes shut tight, then he let out a breath and opened his eyes, staring at her in what looked like wonder.

Her heart filled with warmth and she let herself go liquid against him, dropping to his chest and enjoying the sensation of their chests heaving with rapid breaths. He wrapped his arms around her and held her close, pressing a kiss against the side of her head. She felt him swallow a few times as he caught his breath before speaking.

"You said we could do that again?"

Sylvia felt her lips spread in a broad smile as she laughed.

Chapter Twelve

Light filtered into the cabin from the windows, joining with the golden glow of the fire. Aidan rolled over and reached for Sylvia, but she wasn't there. She must have run to the restroom. From the look of the fire, she had stoked it and added more logs before she left. Her sweats were also gone, which didn't surprise him. The cabin was chilly, even with the fire.

He had lost track of how many times they had made love or how many times he woke as they napped in between to watch her sleep, her back tight against his chest and her hair draped over his arm. He rolled onto his back, smiling up at the ceiling as he studied the Christmas lights. Sylvia had said they should take them down soon, but he was in no rush. The cheerful lights always made him happy. They reminded him of the pixies he spent time with in the woods—tiny magical beings that glowed in every color he'd ever seen on Christmas lights. They could be mischievous to those who crossed them, but Aidan had always considered them friendly companions, if not actual friends. Now, he had Sylvia.

Tonight was New Year's Eve—a powerful time of

transitioning. He would use what magic was left to him to crystalize the spell that had made him human and become fully mortal. He would make sure that he remained Aidan forever, or at least as long as his mortal form lasted. A lifetime with Sylvia was worth it. He'd had enough of immortality if it meant more of being alone. His heart was filled with warmth and hope and… something else. He reached up and rubbed his chest, trying to identify the new emotion on the edge of his awareness.

Purpose. Cold, relentless purpose.

"Sylvia!" Aidan bolted upright just as someone pounded on the front door so hard that the windowpanes rattled.

Sylvia ran out from the corner that led to the bathroom, eyes wide.

"What is it?" she asked, hurrying toward him while she kept glancing over her shoulder at the door. "Is it the Krampus?"

She reached Aidan just as he made it to his feet. The chill in the air tensed his muscles, and he could already feel his teeth start to chatter. Cold mist seeped in under the door, coating the floor near it in a thin layer of snow.

"It has to be," he said.

Sylvia ducked down and grabbed his sweats, then pressed them into his chest. Another knock shook the cabin, light appearing around the edges of the door under the strain. Aidan pulled on his clothing as quickly as he could while Sylvia stood at his side. Snow swirled up the door, the mist rising and wrapping around the doorknob. The locks clicked as they retracted and the door flung itself open.

The Krampus filled the doorway, ducking low to avoid bumping his head on the lintel and turning at an angle to fit his massive shoulders through the space. For a moment, Aidan thought he might be in his polar bear form, but it was just the man, enormous as he was. A blast of cold air entered along with him. Sylvia trembled, wrapping her arms around her middle. She scurried closer to the fire, probably trying to keep from freezing in the presence of the Lord of Endless Snow.

"There you are." The Krampus turned and closed the door behind him, then rose to his full height. He stomped into the great room, snow falling from his shoulders in wet clumps that splatted on the wooden floor. "I've been looking for you."

Before he could reach Aidan, Sylvia leapt between them, swinging the poker from the fireplace. The metal of its tip glowed red-hot, sizzling as it swept through another clump of snow that fell as the Krampus lurched back.

"What the hell?" he said. "Who leaves a poker in the fire?"

"Someone expecting the Lord of Endless Snow to come for the man she loves," Sylvia said.

The man she loves?

Aidan knew what he had sensed from her, what he had seen in her heart. He didn't know she was already prepared to face the deep emotional connection that had been forged between them. His own heart swelled with love, warmth flooding his chest strong enough to fight off Lord Snow's cold.

The Krampus shook his head and swung a massive arm, gesturing toward Aidan. "He's not a man."

"He is now." She looked over at Aidan and held his gaze. "Man enough for me."

"What is it with you mortal women?" The Krampus shook his head, then swirled his finger in the air. A mini snowstorm grew around it, then swept out to surround the poker. The metal cooled to its usual dark color in seconds. He plucked it from her hands as her eyes widened in shock, then set it in its place by the hearth. "If you don't mind, this is Fae business. Not your concern."

"I do mind, and anything involving Aidan is entirely my concern," Sylvia said.

The Krampus narrowed his eyes. "Who?"

"She means me," Aidan said. "I'm not the White Stag anymore. I'm just a man."

The Krampus laughed. "That's a good one. Did you feed that line to her before you hooked up?"

"What do you mean?" Sylvia looked back and forth between them, a sliver of doubt rising in her heart. "What line?"

"I've been nothing but honest with her," Aidan said. He turned to Sylvia and emphatically restated, "With *you*. I still have enough magic in me to read your heart, but I can't grant wishes."

"Not in this form," the Krampus said. "But you will, as soon as I get you changed back."

"No." Sylvia took a few steps forward. "No, you can't turn him back."

"Look, let's all just take a few deep breaths and talk this out like reasonable beings." The Krampus turned to Aidan and said, "We got off on the wrong foot. I was upset and not thinking clearly and my behavior was way over the line. For that, I apologize."

"You apologize?" Aidan said. "You nearly tore my head off."

"Like I said." Krampus made a gesture like he was forming a wall with one hand and used the other to mimic jumping over it as he said, "Over. The line. I just need one wish, and then we can both be on our way."

Aidan shook his head. "I won't. Even if I could, I wouldn't."

The Krampus clasped his hands in front of his body and stood straighter, making himself seem even bigger. "Well, then. We might have a problem."

"Krampus, please," Sylvia pleaded.

"Call me Lord Snow." The Krampus sort of shivered as if trying to shake something off. "Or just Snow. I hate that other name."

"I wondered." She gestured toward him and said, "You don't look like any of the pictures of you that I've seen."

What was she doing, striking up a conversation with him? Aidan could sense her own purpose. She was trying to protect him, to protect their love and the love that the Krampus—Lord Snow—threatened. If Aidan could figure out her plan, maybe he could help with it.

"Those pictures are offensive." Snow shrugged his shoulders as if loosening the pull of his jacket on his massive arms. "And hurtful," he added. "I haven't looked like that since I became the Lord of Endless Snow. That's who I am now. Snow."

"I get it," Sylvia said, nodding with wide eyes. "We will call you Snow."

"Good," he said.

"You'd probably be really upset if you had to turn back," Sylvia said.

"Of course I—" He narrowed his eyes and took a step forward. "Don't try to trick me."

"She's not trying to trick you," Aidan quickly said. "No one is. She's just trying to make a point. I don't want to change back. I want to stay like this forever."

Snow let out a snort. "Forever wouldn't be very long." He gestured toward Sylvia and said, "These mortals rarely last a century."

"I know." Aidan swallowed hard as he gazed at Sylvia.

His chest constricted at the idea of going on without her. "Whatever time I'm given, I want to spend it with her. If I had a wish, that's all I would ask for."

"Aidan…" Sylvia reached for him, clasping his hands and pulling him close. She rose on her tip toes to kiss him, her lips warm and soft.

"Ugh," Snow said, rolling his eyes. "Stop that."

Aidan ignored him, his focus solely on Sylvia as he said, "I love you."

Sylvia's smile was brighter than the Christmas lights. "I love you, too."

"It doesn't matter," Snow said. "This guy—"

"Aidan," Sylvia said, her voice like iron. "We're respecting what you want regarding your name. You need to do the same for us."

"Fine," Snow said, his voice tight. "*Aidan* is the White Stag. He has to return to that form or it will throw off the magical balance. It's already bad enough without a Lord of the North Wind. Losing the White Stag as well would throw the Court of the Yuletide Fae into chaos and make us a target for the other Courts."

"That wouldn't be good," Aidan said, pulling Sylvia against his side.

"No kidding," Snow said.

"But the Winter Queen can choose another Lord of the North Wind," Aidan said.

Snow shook his head and let out a long sigh through

his nose. Aidan didn't think he'd ever heard such a clear sound of exasperation.

"She already has," Snow said. "Jack Frost."

Aidan felt his eyebrows rise. "Jack Frost?"

"He's real, too?" Sylvia said. She shook her head. "What am I saying? Of course, he's real."

"He's real and he's also…" Aidan let his voice trail off, thinking of the few encounters he'd had with Jack Frost and the many, many tales of mischief, frustration, and woe surrounding the fairy.

"He's also a dick," Snow said.

Aidan couldn't argue.

"He's bad enough with his current powers," Aidan said. "If he becomes Lord of the North Wind…" His stomach churned at the thought.

"Which is why I need you back as the White Stag to buy me time to make a case with the Winter Queen to reinstate the Yule Cat as the Lord of the North Wind."

"Aidan…" Sylvia tightened her grip on Aidan's waist. He could sense her fear, a cold coiling in his chest. She turned back to Snow and said, "There has to be another way. A better way."

"I happen to agree."

All three of them started at the cheerful voice coming from somewhere behind Lord Snow. Snow was so huge, he could easily be hiding several people from view. Snow's eyes grew wide as he wheeled around and stepped back, revealing a tall man wearing a red jacket and dark red jeans over gleaming black boots. His fingers were interlaced over his stomach and Aidan could see his smile even through his thick white beard and mustache. His hair was just as snowy white, dusting the tops of his shoulders.

Within his chest, a golden light spread forth, suffusing his entire body with a soft glow that radiated out from him. It was powerful enough to chase the chill away from the room. Joy and love flooded Aidan, so powerful that his knees felt weak. He leaned on Sylvia as she took some of his weight, helping him to remain standing. As if that wasn't wondrous and terrifying enough, Lord Snow—the Krampus—backed away another step.

"I hope you don't mind," the man said. "I let myself in."

"Lord Kringle," Snow said, bowing low.

"No need to be formal." With a beaming smile, Lord Kringle said, "Call me Kris."

Chapter Thirteen

Sylvia let out a laugh as the Krampus—Lord Snow—finally straightened. She'd been doing okay with the idea of fairies and Yule Cats and Krampuses and magic stags, but this? No way. Aidan had said that this particular magical being was real, but it was easier to entertain as a possibility when there wasn't a guy standing in her great room who looked—who *felt*—like this.

"You have got to be kidding me," she said. "There's no way this is Santa."

She glanced up at Aidan to see that his eyes were wide and his mouth slack. Looking at Snow didn't help matters. He was glaring at her like she'd seen celebrity bodyguards do when regular people came too close. His eyes burned red—literally glowing red—and a muscle twitched on his massive jaw. She leaned a little closer to Aidan, which was easy, since he was half-flopping on her.

"People don't respect Father Christmas anymore," Snow said.

"Come now," Kringle said, then somehow managed to pull off a perfect 'ho, ho, ho' laugh without making it sound cheesy or forced.

"They make these weird, cartoony light-up balloons of you and put them in their lawns," Snow said. "It's creepy."

"Oh, I don't know." The famous twinkle sparkled in Kringle's eye. "Have you seen the ones of me riding a dinosaur?" He chuckled and shook his head. "I love those."

"Seriously?" Sylvia said. "*You're* Santa?"

The smile he cast at her somehow flooded her chest with warmth. Her eyes teared up and she had an almost uncontrollable urge to fling her arms around him and give him the biggest hug.

"You can call me Kringle, if you'd rather," Santa said. "But right now, we need to get moving. It's almost midnight, and we're going to need all the juice we can get if we're going to change Aidan back into the White Stag."

Sylvia's heart seemed to freeze in her chest. Her ears rang so loudly from the blood rushing through them that she was certain she had to have heard him wrong. She shook her head as if that would clear it, then wrapped her arms tighter around Aidan's waist.

"You can't," she said. "There's no way Santa would do this. No way he'd separate us."

"Indeed." He had the gall to smile at her, but then he tilted his head forward a bit, so that Snow couldn't see his face, and winked at them. "I'm going to ask you to do something that has been a challenge for you ever since that ex-husband of yours..." He raised his eyebrows. "Well, let's just say 'was exceedingly naughty.' I need you to trust me, Sylvia."

She wasn't sure that she could. She had only just managed to open her heart to Aidan. How could she trust this stranger to somehow manage to change Aidan back without separating them?

"You trust me," Aidan said. He looked down at Sylvia and said, "And I trust him. He said himself he agrees that there's a better way. If anyone can figure it out, it's Lord Kringle."

"Aidan…"

If she lost him, it would be the end of her heart. She would never love anyone again. She knew it in her bones, in her essence. This was her soulmate. She would do anything to be with him. But if there was a hidden cost…

"Is Jack Frost dangerous?" she asked.

"He can be." Aidan nodded. "Mostly when his tricks go sideways. I've never known it to bother him much when it does."

"Then we can't let him become more powerful." She turned to Santa and said, "Okay, what's the plan?"

"First, we need to move outside." He gestured to Snow and said, "If you wouldn't mind? Some proper attire for our friends."

"Of course," Snow said.

Sylvia's heart raced as she wondered what exactly they meant by that and what Snow intended to do. She didn't have to wait long to find out. The massive man lifted one foot, then stomped it down on the floor so hard, she was amazed that it didn't go right through the boards. Instead, a pattern of snowflakes appeared beneath his boot, quickly flowing across the polished oak hardwood toward her and Aidan.

She tried not to flinch as it reached them, but still yelped as the cold crept up their legs. Glancing at Aidan, she saw that he had closed his eyes, but she couldn't bring herself to. She didn't want to miss a moment of this, and as much as she trusted Aidan and was trying to trust Santa, she didn't trust Snow at all.

The snow wrapped around her legs quickly, spreading up over her entire body and encasing her in light and frigid cold. Her body shook with it, arms tightening around Aidan further without thought. The light grew brighter as her sweatpants transformed into snow-white fleece leggings that flared around a pair of matching glossy leather boots, lined with fur and sporting laces that went all the way from her toes to her knees. She felt warm socks encase her feet within them, the fabric softer than anything she'd ever felt before.

Her sweatshirt transformed, flowing down her body as a white dress coat with white wooden clasps in neat double rows up the middle. The neck of it expanded into fur-covered lapels that rested across her collarbones and snugged against her neck, trapping in all her body heat and making her cozy and warm. Matching white gloves spread over her hands, the material soft as kid leather. The snow swirled up through her hair, pleating it into two braids entwined with white ribbon that tied them off. She felt something soft wrap around her head and dared to reach up, finding a soft fur cap on her head. The snow whirled around her once more, then fell to the ground, vanishing as soon as it hit the floor.

"What... I mean... How... That was..." She couldn't find the words to encapsulate her thoughts, which were running crazy anyway. She looked at Aidan and became utterly speechless.

His clothing had also transformed into a similar outfit. The white pants hugged his muscular legs, his jacket stretched across his broad chest and tapered to show off his trim waist, then flared a bit at his hips. Her only complaint was that the length of his coat covered up his backside, but she was sure she could get over it. A soft cap sat on his head, the white fur contrasting brilliantly with his dark hair and the stubble that graced his strong jaw. They looked like they were ready to hit the red carpet or visit royalty in a northern country or something.

"Enough gawking," Snow said. "We're on a tight timeline."

"Wait, this isn't real fur, is it?" Sylvia said, reaching toward her hat as if to remove it.

"Of course not." Snow let out a disgusted grunt. "It's

all magic."

"Oh, okay then," she said.

Something about his indignation was endearing, even with the threat he represented to them. Maybe his heart wasn't as icy as she had originally thought.

"Nicely done," Kringle—Santa—said, beaming at them. He leaned closer to Snow and said, "She'll like this."

"Who will?" Sylvia asked.

For a brief moment, Santa's smile shuttered and his eyes grew unfocused. He opened his mouth a few times, but no words came out. How could a simple question make the man who traveled to every household on Christmas Eve appear so lost? Sylvia took a step toward him, uncertain of what she was about to do, but feeling compelled to comfort him. Snow stepped between them and took a deep breath, puffing up his chest to make himself even bigger than before. She was still wrapping her head around standing in a room with Santa, but had no trouble at all believing that Snow was a polar bear shifter.

"Outside," Snow said gruffly. "Get moving."

Aidan tucked her arm in his elbow and headed for the door. His hand on top of hers was a comfort, though she was still terrified. What was about to happen? The door opened on its own when they approached. Beyond, she could see that the snow had been swept away from her porch. A large area in front of the cabin looked to be covered in packed snow instead of the huge drifts she'd expected.

"Being the Lord of Endless Snow must have its perks," she muttered as they stepped onto the porch.

Snow loomed behind them and leaned down to say, "It does. Now keep moving."

She grimaced at him, but hurried down the steps with Aidan. Above them, the clouds had cleared, leaving an inky black night dotted with diamond-like stars and a bright moon shining above. The light of the full moon caught on the snow in the trees and on the ground, illuminating the entire area with soft white light and making it easy to see everything. The landscape was utterly magical, even without the Fae surrounding her. Her breath came out in puffs of fog, her heart pounding as she worried over what would come next.

Brilliant, tiny lights of all colors flickered into view among the branches, a rainbow of winter fireflies. They floated closer, like the most beautiful Christmas lights that had come to life, filling the clearing with magic. Despite the situation, Sylvia found herself gasping in wonder as they circled around her and Aidan.

"What are these?" she asked.

"Pixies," Aidan said. "They're beautiful, but they can be mischievous, too."

"Most of the Fae can," she agreed. "At least, according to the stories." She turned to Santa and said, "I hope that doesn't apply to you as well."

"Me? Oh no." Santa managed another of those ho-ho-ho laughs in the middle of his sentence. "But I'm a bit different from the others."

"How so?" she asked.

"Enough questions." Snow stepped forward. "Midnight is moments away. Tell me what to do to break the spell keeping Aidan in human form."

"You don't have to do anything," Santa said. "It's all on Aidan. All he has to do is let go."

Aidan's hand tightened around Sylvia's almost enough to hurt. His eyebrows knit together and he shook his head.

"No," he said. "Please, no."

"Wait a minute." Sylvia's heart was pounding, her skin felt electrified. There was no way she was going to sit by and let this happen. "You said there was a better way. You agreed with me."

"A better way than Lord Snow forcing Aidan back into the form of the White Stag." Santa nodded. "There is. He fulfilled your wish and made it so that you could help him, which you've done. And his wish is fulfilled in experiencing what it's like to be human…" There was a wistfulness in his tone as he finished, "if only for a little while."

"No," Sylvia said. "No, you can't take him from me."

"Sylvia." Aidan's voice was painfully gentle.

"No," she said. "If you turn back, the Krampus will use

you to grant his wish. He'll destroy a love. You sensed it. We can't let that happen. And if you turn back—" Her voice broke as tears filled her eyes. "What about us? What about our love? You'll be the White Stag, and I'll just be human."

Aidan cupped her cheek and she shook her head. He leaned in and kissed her, so bittersweet and tender. All his love flowed into her through the kiss, telling her everything they didn't have time to explore, everything he wished they could be and would never have a chance to discover. When he pulled back, a tear spilled from his eye.

"Snow is right," Aidan said. "The balance of power has been thrown off too far. The repercussions could be devastating to so many people, to so many worlds, Fae and mortal alike. There has to be a White Stag."

"Just as there has to be a Lord of the North Wind," Santa said, his booming voice breaking through their moment.

Sylvia looked over to see Santa nudge Snow's arm with his elbow. Snow looked down at him, his eyebrows raised and his mouth hanging open.

He shook his head and said, "No. Absolutely not."

Santa sort of shrugged, then turned to her and winked again. She didn't know what was going on, but she had a sense that it was important. Incredibly important. She struggled to find a way to help.

"Is that any way to talk to Lord Kringle?" she said.

Snow scowled at her, but then turned back to Santa and bowed. "With all due respect, I've been given orders—"

"That you have already disobeyed." Santa clucked his tongue. "That was a bit naughty of you."

Snow blinked a few times, then ran his hand over the close-cropped hair on his scalp. He walked a few steps away from Santa, shaking his head.

"All I wanted was for my family to be whole again," Snow said.

Santa nodded. In a gentle voice, he said, "That is a wish we share. But if you want to bring people together, you can't do so by driving them apart."

Snow let out a sigh that seemed to drop the temperature around them another dozen degrees. Even with her warm gear, Sylvia shivered. Her heart was racing as she wondered what exactly was going on. She didn't dare ask, seeing the turmoil in Snow's features. She had to… to trust Santa.

How has my life become this strange?

"If we're going to do this, we need to do it now," Santa said, his voice softer. "And if she has a problem with it, she's welcome to take it up with me."

Sylvia didn't know who they were talking about. She was the only 'she' in the clearing. Stepping closer to them, she kept a firm grip on Aidan's hand as she said, "If there's anything you can do to keep Aidan and me together, please do it. I don't care what it is, as long as it doesn't hurt anybody else."

"There isn't a way for no one to be hurt." Aidan stared at Snow as he said, "That's the real reason behind your wish. You want North back as your partner in the Yuletide Kingdom. You miss him and want things to go back to the way they were."

That's what this was about? Aidan had told her that Snow and North were like brothers, but that North had found love with a human woman. She had only been happy for North, not thinking of how it would affect Snow. When she was younger, she had always believed that bringing in someone to love made a family bigger, it didn't split them apart. But she knew from bitter experience that wasn't always the case. If North was no longer Lord of the North Wind, did that meant he had left Snow behind?

Snow's eyes began to glow red again. His chest heaved with quick breaths as white light enveloped him. The light grew, burning her eyes and changing his silhouette, then finally vanishing to leave behind an enormous polar bear. Mist rose from his pelt and snowflakes swirled around him as he let out a roar that shook the trees, dislodging huge clumps of snow that splatted to the ground.

"Now, Snow," Santa said, stepping between them.

Sylvia released Aidan's hand and ran forward. She ducked past Santa and plowed right into Snow's furry belly, wrapping her arms around him as far as she could. A tremor flowed through him as she tightened her embrace.

"I'm so sorry," she said. "I'm sorry that he left you to be with someone else. But if he really is like a brother to you, that doesn't mean you've lost him. That doesn't mean you can't figure out a way to still be close. To be family." She leaned back so that she could look up into Snow's startled, glowing eyes. "And I swear to you, I will do everything I can to help you find that new path. Even if you have to turn Aidan back into the White Stag, you don't have to destroy North's love to be part of his life. You don't have to use your wish for that."

Snow let out a sigh that rustled her hair. She felt his paws on her back and tensed, wondering if he was about to tear her apart for daring to speak to him the way she was, to hug him. Honestly, she couldn't believe that she'd done it herself. All she had known was the pain that she finally understood. The pain that connected them. The urge to do something to ease his suffering had blinded her to anything else. Now, looking into the eyes of the giant, magical polar bear that was the Krampus, she wondered if that impulse would cost her everything.

He let out another sigh, his breath becoming more even. His skin rippled beneath her arms as a softer light covered him. The soft fur brushing against her retreated into his form as he shrank down to his still enormous—but on a human scale—size. His arms remained around her.

"Dammit," he muttered under his breath. "Go on. Go stand by your man, for as long as you can call him that."

Her heart started to pound again. This was it, then. He was going to turn Aidan back. But as she turned to go to Aidan, she realized that Snow held on for just a moment longer than she expected. He was hugging her back, not just leaving his arms where they'd been. She glanced up at him, and swore she saw a slight smile as he finally let her go.

Sylvia hurried to Aidan's side. He was staring at her with the same wonder that he'd shown to Santa when he first arrived.

"What?" she said.

"I can't believe you did that." Aidan smiled at her, tucking her arm into his elbow once more and resting his hand on hers. "I am… so honored that you've chosen to share your incredible heart with me."

"For as long as it lasts," she murmured and instantly regretted it when Aidan's smile faltered.

"Let's do this." Snow nodded at Santa, coming to stand by his side. "With the power of the new year, the full moon, and both of us working together, we should be able to manage it."

"Sounds like you have a new plan." Santa chuckled and winked at Snow.

Snow shook his head, then clapped his hands together. A circle of light burst into view at the edges of the clearing, with Aidan and Sylvia at its center. He gripped her hands tightly, staring into her eyes as the light crept closer.

In a strong voice, Snow began to speak. "As the clock strikes midnight with the changing of the year, two souls stand before me, human and deer."

"Aidan…" Sylvia stepped closer to Aidan as the light formed a silhouette of golden antlers that rose from his head. He was turning back. She blinked away her tears and forced herself to smile. "You have opened my heart to love again. And all the love I have, I give to you. For as much time as we have. I love you. Forever."

"I love you, too," he said. "Forever."

Aidan's face elongated back to the snout of his deer form as the light seeped deeper into his body. His skin paled as it turned back to his white pelt. His hands fell away from hers as they turned to hooves, his legs and arms straightening into those of a stag's. For a moment, despair washed through her as she remembered how happy it had made him to be able to hold her in his arms. He would never be able to do that to someone again. Never hold anyone close.

How could this be the better way? The better plan? The light warmed her, spreading over her skin and soaking into her muscles and bones. She wasn't sure what it was doing to her, but she didn't care. She only wished there was a way for them to be together. She closed her eyes and imagined each moment when Aidan had held her in his arms, replaying each heated kiss, each tender moment. A wave of dizziness assailed her and she fell forward onto her hands and… feet? Her head was oddly heavy.

She heard Santa say, "Finish it, son," before Snow spoke again.

"Aidan, I no longer call you foe. White Stag, I give to you the White Doe."

Her eyes flew open to see Aidan staring at her with his wide golden eyes, his antlers glowing gold and his pelt gleaming in the moonlight. He stamped his front leg and shook his head, then let out a bellow that made her heart race with excitement. She wanted to run into the forest, to leap into the air and fly up to the stars above them. Anticipation of their run heated her blood as she stamped her arm… her foot… her… hoof?

What did Lord Snow say before? The White Doe?

She curved her neck to look at her body, her head heavy with a strange weight. Her body was covered in a coat of white, four long, slender legs stretched beneath her to the ground, and a tail flicked on her rump. She was a deer! She turned back to Aidan and made the most bizarre noise she'd ever heard. It was the closest thing to a laugh she could manage. If this meant they could be together, so be it. She would miss being human, but it was worth it to be with him.

Aidan stepped forward and nuzzled the side of her head with his. She felt her antlers bump against his, though they felt smaller. That was probably for the best as she became used to her new form. She tried to take a step and stumbled, but Aidan was there to help her keep to her feet —all four of them.

They both turned toward Snow and Santa, the one looking grumbly and the other beaming with a smile. This must have been Santa's plan all along. Sylvia wished that he had asked her first. She would have said yes, but it would have been nice to have an idea of what to expect. An odd thought popped into her head that she and Aidan could join Santa's reindeer at Christmastime and she let out another of the odd bugling laughs.

Santa joined her, then nudged Snow again. "And the last part. The new year is upon us. A time of growth and hope. A time of change."

Snow sighed, then nodded. He turned toward them and lifted both arms. Once again, the circle flared with light. This time, a whirlwind of snow rose with it. She had to close her eyes against the driving flakes. Aidan pressed his flank against hers, shielding her as best he could. At least she didn't feel the cold anymore. Still, her heart thudded, her new instincts screaming at her to run.

I trust them. I choose to trust them. I choose to open my heart to love, even with its risks.

The wind whipped against them, infusing her with an energy unlike anything she had ever felt before. Her muscles sang with it, her mind opened to possibilities she had never entertained. Flight would be nothing. Stepping between worlds an afterthought. The universe shifted and made sense in ways her mortal mind could never have comprehended.

My mortal mind… is gone…

In that moment, she knew she had become something else. Even before Snow finished, with, "Now you are my kith and kin—Lord and Lady of the North Wind."

Chapter Fourteen

The moment the wind had touched his pelt, Aidan knew it carried great power. He never would have dreamed it carried the power of the Lord of the North Wind, nor that Snow was planning on dividing that power between Sylvia and himself. It made sense, though. Even with the magic of the turning of the New Year, he wouldn't have been strong enough to turn Aidan back if Aidan had fought him. He certainly wouldn't have been able to turn Sylvia into the White Doe.

He had felt Lord Snow and Lord Kringle's powers drawing on his own, along with the powerful magic of that moment and place, but had no idea what their plan was. Aidan looked over at Sylvia, his heart filled with worry. She hadn't agreed to this. They should have asked her. Being together as humans was so different than being together as deer. Would she even want this? He hated that he couldn't just ask her, but in these forms, they couldn't speak.

I said I wanted them to do whatever it took to keep us together, and I meant it.

He felt his eyes widen as he stepped closer to her. *I can*

hear your thoughts! Can you hear mine?

I can. She nodded, the small antlers on her head glinting gold in the moonlight.

He wished she could see his smile, but that was another thing that would be hard to do in these forms. Instead, he nuzzled the side of her head again.

"The plan is not complete," Snow said, trudging toward them, his voice a low rumble. "Whatever you do, do not run. That would be very annoying."

Sylvia's muscles twitched beneath her pelt. The instinct to flee was hardwired into these forms, especially when confronted with such a powerful predator. She took a step back, but her legs went every which way. Aidan tried to keep her from falling again, but he didn't have arms to catch her and this was so much worse than before. She ended up splayed in the snow.

She let out a heavy sigh. *I thought deer were supposed to be naturally graceful.*

Aidan filled his mind with reassuring laughter. *You're a magical deer, not a natural one. But think of the perks.*

Such as?

Flight? Immortality?

It had only just hit him in that moment. Yes, they had lost a lot by taking these forms, but she was immortal now, as he was. They would have eternity together to explore the worlds. He couldn't wait to teach her everything he knew about the Faerie realms and show her all of their wonders.

I would share your excitement, but Snow is still heading our way, she thought.

He turned just as Snow arrived. Aidan held very, very still, though his own instincts screamed for him to run. Sylvia wouldn't be able to keep up. He couldn't leave her behind.

Snow shook his head, then reached down and plucked Sylvia from the snow, setting her on her feet. He kept his hands on her sides till she was steady.

"Just give me a minute before you try to walk or anything," he said.

Now that they were calmer, Aidan could better sense his heart. There was an emptiness there that had scared him before. Now that he knew its source, he was sure that he and Sylvia could help him. What made Aidan's muscles calm and his heart slow to a steadier beat was the one thing he hadn't seen before in Snow's heart—hope.

"I'll take that wish now," Lord Snow said.

Aidan blinked, but then nodded and lowered his head in a bow. Snow sucked in a quick breath, as if surprised. Beside him, Sylvia bent her front knees as if also trying to bow, but her legs wobbled and she started to fall again. Snow caught her easily and stood her back up.

"What did I say about not trying to move?" He let out a frustrated grunt, shaking his head, but his expression softened when she nuzzled his cheek with her nose.

Aidan didn't know what Snow's wish would be. He was surprised he still wanted one, after everything that had happened. But Aidan had asked Sylvia to trust Snow and Kringle. Aidan would do the same. He stood still, waiting for Snow to grip his antlers and make his wish. Instead, Snow spoke again.

"You know, when the Winter Queen found me, I had one friend in all the worlds. North. He was in his Yule Cat form all the time then. We each only had the one form. Nobody wanted to be near me, the way I looked before." He shook his head and sighed. "It was so hard to help people. But the Queen knew we could help. We could do more, if we had the right tools, the right powers, the right forms."

Aidan's heart seemed to pause, then it pounded in his chest as hope flooded him. What was Snow about to do?

"As Lord and Lady of the North Wind, you're going to need to be able to give guidance to your subjects," Snow said. "You need to be able to represent the Yuletide Kingdom in our affairs with the other Courts. You can't do it like this and you can't do it if you're constantly being hunted. I can't make people stop chasing you…" A huge grin stretched his face, his eyes crinkling up at the edges. "But I can make them really, really sorry when they catch you."

He reached up and placed one hand on Aidan's antlers and the other on Sylvia's. "My wish is for the both of you to become shifters, like North and me, but more. To have the ability to take on any form that you want or need for a given situation. Maybe you'll be deer most of the time. I'm guessing a lot of your time will be spent in human form. But I am very curious to see what else you'll get up to, especially when the next jackass comes around looking for a wish that shouldn't be granted."

Aidan's heart swelled in his chest. His eyes glazed over, blurring his vision as the greatest gratitude he had ever felt filled his body. He didn't have to look at Sylvia to know she felt the same. Their link let him feel it, her own joy was flooding through him. This was a wish he could wholeheartedly grant. Sylvia would be safe from hunters. They both would be. And they could be together. He could hold her again.

He let his joy grow within him, his power rising as the wish unfolded, mirrored in Sylvia's new powers. Their antlers glowed beneath Snow's hands, the golden light spreading over their bodies and filling the clearing as bright as a summer day. He felt his muscles shifting once more, his coat retreating. As their antlers shrank back into them, Snow's hands were drawn along with them, leaving his large palms on the sides of their heads.

Aidan looked down to see that he was back in his human form, wearing the outfit Snow had made for him. He turned to see Sylvia in her human form and snow gear as well. Her eyes were wide and flooding with tears as she smiled up at Snow. To Aidan's amazement, Snow returned her smile, warmth and affection flowing out from him.

"Thank you," she said, then threw her arms around his middle again.

"Lord Snow…" Aidan began.

"Ahh, come on." Snow shook his head, then wrapped his big arms around them both, lifting them from the ground. He squeezed them hard enough that Aidan could barely breathe, but Sylvia's reassuring laugh made him join in.

"Now, that worked out quite well, I think," Kringle said from behind them.

Snow turned and set them on the ground. The moment their feet touched the earth, Sylvia reached out and took Aidan's hand in hers, smiling up at him.

"This was your plan all along," Aidan said to Lord Kringle. "To have Snow use his wish to make us shifters after giving us the power of the North Wind so that Sylvia could become like me."

Kringle shrugged, his smile making the corners of his eyes crinkle.

"That plan had a lot of moving parts," Sylvia said. "A lot of risk."

"Not at all," Kringle said, gazing at Snow fondly. "I know Lord Snow quite well. I know his heart, as I know all of yours. As I know everyone's."

A cloud passed over his own heart briefly, some

sadness that had touched him deeply flitting through his mind. Sylvia's grip tightened on Aidan's hand, and he knew she had sensed it, too. They both took a step forward, wanting to help if they could, but Santa raised a hand and shook his head.

"Now, now," he said. "You have much to do and even more to learn. Sylvia must master her deer form, and you must both learn what it means to be Lord and Lady of the North Wind. The Winter Queen… Well, she likes things just so, isn't that right, Lord Snow?"

"Yes, it is," Snow said, nodding. "We need to train you before we present you to the Queen. That will take time, but if we mess up, she'll exile us all and replace us with jerks like Jack Frost."

"And she doesn't like to be kept waiting," Santa said. He made a point of schooling his expression in thought. "Aidan can help with the deer form, but the powers of the North Wind… Perhaps you'll need the help of an expert? Someone who has already filled the role?"

Aidan smiled as he turned to Snow. "It'll be a great opportunity for you to bond with North as he is now. Just the Yule cat."

"And we'll be there with you to support you every step of the way," Sylvia added.

Snow nodded, then rested his large hands on their shoulders. "Then it's time for your first lesson as the Lord and Lady of the Yuletide Court."

"What's that?" Sylvia asked.

Smiling, he said, "Portals."

Chapter Fifteen

Sylvia sat at one of the tables in The Yuletide Bakery. It wasn't her usual spot at the two-seater in the corner, out of everyone's way. She was right in the center, at the biggest table they had, and every chair was filled. Snow took up two seats as he shook his head and laughed at yet another hilarious story North Cotter, no longer Lord of the North Wind, was sharing with them all. Those two had really been up to some mischief in the millennia of their existence.

Melanie, the human woman North had fallen in love with, kept running back and forth from the kitchen to the bakery, bringing them more cookies and pastries, while North kept their cups filled with coffee or cocoa or tea. Sylvia had offered to help, but they definitely already had a routine going, and with the bakery closed for the New Year's Day holiday, they had the place to themselves. Melanie had also shared that Santa had given her the gift of immortality, technically making her one of the Fae, just as Sylvia was.

She still couldn't believe it. She was the White Doe, whatever that meant. Would she be able to grant wishes?

Would she be forced to? The powers that Snow had given them were beyond what she could conceive of at the moment. Then again, the powers of the North Wind were nothing to mess around with, either.

A few times, the napkins at the table had begun to stir as she or Aidan became too carried away with their stories. North had been quick to jump in and coach them through the moments, but there had still been an incident or two when cups were overturned and napkins blew away. She had so much to learn, but then, she had forever to learn it.

Aidan smiled over at her, squeezing her hand that he held under the table, their fingers interlaced. His love flowed through her, reminding her that she wouldn't be alone in this. She would never be alone again.

I'm not the only reason you won't be alone, he thought. He nodded toward the table, bringing her attention back to the people sitting around it.

"Hey, we're out of cookies." Snow held up a massive plate that only held crumbs.

"I'll go get more," Melanie said, rising. A glowing golden pixie flitted around her head, following as she headed toward the kitchen. Just another magical thing that everyone treated as everyday in the bakery.

"I'll help so we can put a few more batches in the ovens." North took the plate and nudged Snow with his shoulder. "This one is a bottomless pit."

"Ehh." Snow 'nudged' him back, sending North

staggering a few paces. Both men grinned.

When they were alone, Sylvia reached out with her free hand and grasped Snow's hand that was resting on the table.

"I don't feel like I've properly thanked you," she said.

Snow shrugged. "You did. But, hey, I made out on the deal. I have the White Stag. I have a Lord and Lady of the North Wind to present to the Winter Queen—when you're ready. And best of all, I don't have to work with that jackass, Frost."

Sylvia shook her head, sensing that he was deflecting the greater part of the emotions roiling through him. She had gained the same ability to read hearts that Aidan had when she'd been made his counterpart as the White Doe. Snow was concerned about his choices. He worried about how the Winter Queen might react to him not obeying her command. He had taken a huge risk for them.

Sylvia squeezed his hand, and said, "You gave me all these powers and immortality and a chance to be with the love of my life." She turned to smile at Aidan, his love warming her. Addressing Snow again, she said, "But there's something else I haven't thanked you for yet."

"What's that?" Snow asked, one eyebrow arched as genuine curiosity flowed from him.

"You brought me into your family," she said. "A family like I've always dreamed of having. And any sort of family isn't something I've had for a long time."

He tightened his grip on her hand and nodded tersely. "No one should be without a family. Least of all someone with a heart as warm as yours."

His eyes widened and he looked away, embarrassment edging out the curiosity from just before. Sylvia rose up from her seat and wrapped her arms around Snow's neck, giving him a huge hug. He stiffened at first, then chuckled, patting her back as he returned her hug.

The door to the kitchen opened, and she heard North say, "Are we missing out on hugs?"

Sylvia stood straighter, but left one arm around Snow's shoulders. She smiled at Aidan, then glanced down to point out that Snow had left one arm around her waist as well.

"This guy gives the best hugs in all the worlds, you know," North said, setting another huge plate of cookies in front of them before pulling out Melanie's chair. "At least, when he means it."

"There's a reason bear hugs are so famous," Snow said and chuckled.

They all joined in, laughter ringing through the space. Sylvia's heart was filled with such warmth, she thought she might burst. The wind picked up, stirring her hair, but she was able to calm it herself this time. Aidan nodded, his face beaming with pride as he rose and stood by her side, wrapping an arm around her shoulders as she clasped his waist with her free arm.

Thanks to a New Year's wish and so many people being willing to trust each other, this was her future. A place where she belonged with friends, family, and the most magical gift of all. True love.

Epilogue

Snow set out down the sidewalk, heading toward his closest home, not far from the Yuletide Bakery. He needed to contact Malachi, the steward who was acting in Snow's place while he was in the mortal realm, and check on the newest members of his Court. There were many things to keep moving in the Yuletide Kingdom. Snow looked forward to when Aidan and Sylvia would be ready to assist him with them. They were almost there.

Snow had to believe he had made the right choice. Otherwise, what he had done was certain to get him banished form the Yuletide Kingdom. The idea of working with Frost, giving that jackass more power... Snow would never regret making Aidan and Sylvia the Lord and Lady of the North Wind. Snow just had to figure out what his next move was.

How could he spin this so that the Winter Queen wouldn't banish all of them and take back the powers she had given them? At least she couldn't take the powers granted by Snow's wish for Aidan and Sylvia. He was comforted in knowing they would be safe.

"Well, well, well," an obnoxious voice said. "Look what the cat dragged down to his rebellious level."

Snow's skin prickled with the urge to take on his polar bear form, turn around, and in one fluid movement knock the speaker's head from his shoulders. He took a deep breath and let it out slow, forcing himself to calm. Glancing over his shoulder, he saw Jack Frost sitting on a mailbox, one knee raised and the other dangling over its side.

"What do you want, Frost?" Snow asked.

"What do I want?" He pressed his fingertips against his chest, his ice-blue eyes widening in mock surprise. "Wow, it's so kind of you to ask. Let's see, what *do* I want?"

"I have stuff to do." Snow shook his head and continued down the street.

"Stuff like defying the Queen?"

Snow stopped, fists clenching at his sides. Frost slid from the mailbox, then turned and kicked it over.

"That's a felony," Snow said.

"Like I care about mortal laws or mortal…" he waved his fingers in the air dismissively "anything."

The more he talked, the more certain Snow became that he had done the right thing. He walked back to the mailbox and righted it, picking up the letters that had spilled from it and tucking them into the box.

"How very civic-minded of you," Frost said. "If only

you had half as much respect for the rule of the Winter Queen."

"Keep talking," Snow said. "I'm pretty sure I can shove you into that mailbox, too."

Frost snorted. "You could always mail me to Kringle. Maybe he has an opening since you just gave away what is rightfully mine. And to that dumb deer-guy and his previously mortal whatever-she-is?"

"Watch it," Snow said. "They'll be a thousand-fold better at being Lord and Lady of the North Wind than you would be."

"That wasn't for you to decide," Frost snapped.

Rage twisted his features into a dark maelstrom, his black eyebrows arcing on his forehead, his eyes glowing livid blue as the sound of crackling ice spread from where he stood. A blast of frost shot out from his body, enveloping Snow in a thick coat of cold. Snow smirked, then stomped a foot, the frost falling harmlessly to the ground.

"Neat trick," Snow said. "Kinda tickled. I'm the Lord of Endless Snow, remember?"

Frost stepped forward, then blurred, appearing right in Snow's face. Well, a foot down from it. Snow didn't flinch. Frost stared at him balefully for a few moments before his features reverted to their usual appearance. He smiled.

"I'm a pain in the ass on a good day, right?" Frost said.

Snow shrugged, but nodded.

"And that's when I'm being my usual playful, whimsical self," Frost said. His features darkened slightly as he continued. "Just imagine what I can be like when I'm *pissed off.*" He shook himself and smiled again, then reached up and straightened Snow's jacket. "You won't have to imagine for long."

In a puff of cold mist, he disappeared.

Snow stood on the sidewalk for a few moments. It wasn't that he was worried about Frost. That blowhard wouldn't be able to touch Snow. But he could cause trouble for the people Snow cared about, both in the Yuletide Kingdom and in the mortal realm.

Snow needed to get Aidan and Sylvia firmly set in their places as Lord and Lady of the North Wind. He needed the Winter Queen to recognize them to keep them safe from Frost and others that would come running at the first sign of weakness. Their training had gone well with North's help. They couldn't delay it any more. It was time to go home.

—

Thank you so much for reading *The White Stag!* This trilogy has become one of my own comfort reads, and this book is especially tender for me. I hope it brought you joy and laughter and can't wait to share with you what happens next!

The magic comes full circle in the final book of the trilogy, *The Krampus*. I have so much in store for Lord Snow before he reaches his own "happily ever after." Read on to see how the Krampus fares when he introduces the new Lord and Lady of the North Wind to the Winter Queen!

The Krampus

Court of the Yuletide Fae
Book Three

Chapter One

Five weeks, two days, eleven hours, and thirty-five minutes. Lord Snow was ready to go home. While the mortal realm wasn't quite the pit that most of the Fae thought, Snow still didn't want to hang around any longer than he had to. They called him 'the Krampus,' by the Gods' sake, and made up horrible stories about him. *Him* —the Lord of Endless Snow. Why would he want to stick around a place like that?

In front of him, his best friend, North snuck up behind his mate, Melanie, and wrapped his arms around her waist to pull her against his chest in a hug. She laughed and swatted at him, trying to arrange a plate of cookies in their bakery. Snow's newest friends, Aidan and Sylvia—also known as the White Stag and… the Fae Lady soon to be known as the White Doe, once Snow spread the word—watched on, also laughing. Aidan darted forward and snatched a handful of the cookies, earning him a playful swat of his own from Melanie and a look of reproach.

Snow's heart ached oddly and he rubbed the spot. It felt hollow, like something was missing in his chest. The mortal realm often had this effect on him. He didn't like it. The longer they stayed, the stronger the feeling became. He was certain it would also make it harder for Aidan and Sylvia to leave. Between all that and the threat presented by Fae coveting Aidan and Sylvia's power…

"It's time," Snow said, his voice calm and low.

The others froze in place, their smiles falling. Aidan and Sylvia looked to each other and nodded, but Melanie rushed forward.

"It's too soon," she said. "They need more training."

Snow shook his head. "They're more than ready. The longer we wait, the more angry the Winter Queen will become at our absence."

"All the more reason to—"

"Melanie," Sylvia said. "It's okay. Really, it's okay."

She looked to Snow with a smile that echoed through the hollowness in his chest. At least it also warmed the space. "If Snow says we're ready, we're ready."

North pulled Aidan into an embrace and clapped the man on the back. "Remember everything I taught you. You'll be a fine Lord of the North Wind."

"I learned from the best," Aidan said.

Melanie's eyes filled with tears, but she forced herself to smile as she hugged Sylvia as well. "You'll come visit me, right?"

"As often as I can." Sylvia kissed Melanie's dark hair before pulling back.

All of them had become so close during their training. Snow hated to separate Aidan and Sylvia from their friends, but it was inevitable. If things went well, they would be able to come and go from the mortal realm whenever they liked. If things didn't go well…

This will work. It has to work.

Snow had several contingency plans, each more desperate than the last. He was certain he wouldn't have to use any of them. He stood straighter, exuding confidence to help inspire the others. Aidan caught his eyes and nodded, then offered his arm to Sylvia. The pair approached Snow with perfect posture, shoulders back and heads held high like the Fairy Lord and Lady that they had become. Snow smiled down at them, then pulled them into a hug. He was so proud of all they had done.

The Winter Queen would accept them. He was sure of it.

Being back in the Yuletide Kingdom wasn't as comforting as Snow had expected. The castle seemed bigger and much, much colder. Cold couldn't affect him physically. Snow wondered at the chill that settled in his heart. He led Aidan and Sylvia toward the throne room, taking one last moment to glance at their attire and make sure the magical clothes he had fashioned for them were acceptable.

Sylvia's red hair gleamed against the white gown she wore. The fabric sparkled with diamonds that shined in the light cast from the crystal walls of the castle. A mesh of platinum chains held her hair in a chignon and a white silk cape lined with gray-specked fur was fastened around her shoulders.

Aidan wore a similar cape, along with a princely jacket that fit his new station. Or at least the station that Snow was hoping he would soon officially be bestowed. His dark hair was a sharp contrast to the white clothing Snow had created for him.

"You're going to do great," Snow said quietly as they entered the room. "Just remember everything I taught you."

The entire castle and everything in it had been grown from magical crystal that glowed from within, granting a soft light to the space. The Winter Queen sat on her crystal throne in the middle of a raised dias at one side of the room. Usually, two ornate thrones sat at her sides, one for Lord Snow and the other for Lord North. Today, there were none. Snow led Aidan and Sylvia to the center of the room, then approached the Queen's throne and bowed deeply.

After a silence that stretched on for several minutes, the Winter Queen said, "Lord Snow, you have been gone longer than expected. I had begun to wonder if you, too, had abandoned me."

"Never, my Queen," Snow said, rising to meet her gaze. "I regret that it took me so long to succumb to your wisdom. I see now that North is lost to us."

His stomach churned with nerves. Did she know that North was still the Yule Cat? And that Snow had defied her decrees in so many other ways? He was certain that she would be happy with the outcome of his choices eventually, but not so sure she could forgive his willingness to go against what she had proclaimed.

"I have done as you said and brought back the Lord of the North Wind," Snow said.

He swallowed hard, hoping fervently that she would accept Aidan and Sylvia. If the Queen rejected them, he would protect them. Any punishment would fall on his shoulders alone. He'd make sure of it.

"Yet I do not see Jack Frost." She looked pointedly over the heads of Aidan and Sylvia.

"True, but I bring another." He gestured toward Aidan. "I present to you the new Lord and Lady of the North Wind."

Aidan bowed low and Sylvia curtseyed, both of them holding the positions of deference, their eyes cast down to the floor.

"You present to me the new Lord and Lady of the North Wind?" the Winter Queen parroted. "Their manners are better than the last 'new Lady' you brought before me, but that hardly makes up for defying my commands. I know that North remains the Yule Cat. And now you have taken the power I entrusted to you and placed it within these people who are unknown to me."

"Majesty, I beg your forgiveness," Snow said, bowing lower than before. "I could not bring myself to take away the essence that North was born with. He has been the Yule Cat for as long as I have been... the Krampus." He hated claiming the name, but knew the import for this moment. "When you found us, you saw potential and gifted us with power to serve you better, to serve the Yuletide Kingdom. I believe that North can yet be of service to us, but this pair will be an even better Lord and Lady of the North Wind."

"And why would you think that?" she asked in an

imperious voice.

Snow stood, then nodded to Aidan and Sylvia, stepping away. Aidan took Syvlia's hand and nodded to her as well, no doubt encouraging her. She was trembling slightly from nerves. The cold would no longer affect her after the powers Snow had granted to her—some of which she was better at using than others. Reading people's hearts had come instinctively. Shifting and controlling her new form… She was still getting used to that.

White light covered their bodies, suffusing them until they were merely silhouettes. Their shapes changed, antlers sprouting from their heads, faces becoming muzzles, and bodies falling forward onto four legs as they assumed their deer forms. The light withdrew, but they were still white as snow, their coats gleaming with radiance. Their antlers were gold and put off their own light, as did their golden eyes.

The Winter Queen's eyes widened as she rose from the throne, her hands clasped tightly in front of her. She took a step forward, then another and another. When she reached the steps, she hurried down them, approaching the White Stag and the White Doe with what Snow hoped was wonder in her eyes. She reached out to touch them, and Snow held his breath. Though Aidan and Sylvia were skittish in this form, neither flinched as the Winter Queen rested her hands on their muzzles.

"Oh, Krampus," the Queen said, a wistful note to her

voice that he had never heard before. "You have done well."

She continued to hold both Sylvia and Aidan's faces, even going so far as to stroke their foreheads lightly. Snow couldn't believe the wonder in her gaze as she looked at them. His heart gave a little tug as he realized he had never seen her truly happy. Not like he'd seen North and Melanie be. Or Aidan and Sylvia. For the briefest moment, Snow wondered what that would feel like for himself. He quickly buried the thought.

"You will be wondrous additions to my court," the Queen said, resting one of her hands on each of the deers' cheeks.

Her expression clouded, her eyebrows pinching together and her smile fading as she stepped back, pulling her hands away as if startled. Aidan followed, as did Sylvia. Krampus was about to intervene, uncertain of what was going on, but all they did was gently bump their noses against her arms. The Queen's lips tightened and she pulled her fisted hands up to her heart, holding them there like a shield.

Aidan dropped to his knees in a cumbersome bow for his present stag form. He bowed his head so low that his nose touched the ground. Sylvia looked over at him, then made a disgruntled squeak. Her legs shook as she maneuvered herself into a position they had never practiced in this form.

Sylvia stared at the knees of her forelegs—which did not bend at all the way her elbows did when those limbs were arms—then let out a sigh and started to lower herself. Snow held his breath to see if she could manage it. At first, it looked as though she would make it, but then she started to lose her balance. Aidan began to rise, but it was the Queen who reached Sylvia first.

The tall woman launched forward, wrapping her arms around Sylvia's chest and righting her. Together, the women lowered themselves to the ground. Syvlia's ears flicked with interest as she looked up into the Queen's wide green eyes. The doe bowed her head in the Queen's embrace.

"You may be in the form that is of greatest comfort to you, child," the Queen said in a gentle voice.

Light swept over Sylvia as she reverted to her human form. She was still on all fours on the floor. Snow wanted to cover his eyes and shake his head, but he also couldn't tear himself away from the scene unfolding before him. The Queen kept her hold on Sylvia, grasping her elbows and helping her rise amid the voluminous folds of her gown.

The Queen glanced at Snow as they rose, her cheeks actually flushing pink for the first time—in his presence at least. This was so much better than he had even hoped. The Queen was not only accepting Aidan and Sylvia, but seemed delighted by them. He was well on his way to bringing his family back together again. He just had to get the Queen to forgive North for choosing Melanie over her.

The Queen turned to Aidan and said, "You as well, Lord North."

Snow's cheeks pinched as he felt the biggest smile he'd ever had stretch his face. She had accepted Aidan. Snow was sure she would accept Sylvia, too. Aidan glowed brightly as he rose up on his back legs, resuming his human form. He bowed again, and the Queen angled her head toward him in response.

She pulled Sylvia up the steps of the dais with her. As they approached the throne, two more chairs grew from the crystal floor—smaller, of course, but just as ornate and beautiful. Snow felt his mouth drop open as the Queen swirled her finger and a cushion appeared on the chair at her left. She set Sylvia on it, then turned to Aidan and gestured him toward the other seat. With a quick glance to Snow, Aidan hurried after them. He didn't sit until the Queen did.

Snow's heart was pounding in his throat. She had definitely accepted them, but there was a coldness in her bearing as she looked at him. His misgiving grew when she turned to him with a distinct frown.

"You have done well in bringing me my new Lord North and Lady... Silver," the Queen said. "But that does not excuse your defiance. I had expected Jack Frost to be among my court."

Snow opened his mouth to say something, but snapped it shut. Sylvia was squirming in her seat, obviously also wanting to jump in, but they had gone over this time and again. The Queen had a temper that burned icy hot. It was best not to get in the way of it.

He dropped to one knee, bowing his head deeply. "Majesty, I beg your forgiveness," he said.

Silence drew on in the room. Snow's heart was a constant drumbeat in his ears. If she exiled him, as she had North, then Aidan and Sylvia would be on their own navigating their new duties. He didn't want that for them. Snow knew that his subjects could keep things running. He had trained them well. But this was his home. He had done all of this because the Queen and her court and all their subjects were his family. He didn't want to lose that.

"Forgiveness is something that takes time," she said, her voice barely above a whisper. "And sometimes distance as well."

Was she banishing him? He wasn't sure. Her demeanor was so unlike what he was used to. Again, the silence stretched on.

"Lord Snow," she said.

He closed his eyes and let out a huge breath, the tension that knotted his back eased somewhat. She still called him 'Lord Snow.' He wasn't being banished.

"Return to the mortal realm," she said. "I will summon you to return when I am ready."

When would that be? How long did she need him to stay away? She hadn't said he couldn't contact anyone in the Yuletide Kingdom, so he would be able to check in with his seneschals, but still… His mind filled with a thousand questions, scenarios, and endless lists of tasks to keep things running well. It had been him alone for so long while North was in exile—an exile Snow had hoped to ease, not share.

"Majesty, if I may?" Sylvia said in a gentle voice.

Snow's heart sank. He didn't want her to get in the middle of this. Things were going too well for them. He didn't dare look up, but he heard the swish of fabric as Sylvia approached him. She wrapped her arms around his shoulders, her hug bringing her lips close to his ear.

"We'll be okay, you can trust us," she whispered. "Just give her the time she needs." Sylvia rose and returned to her spot at the Queen's side.

"You are kind," the Queen said. "As I can be as well."

"Of course, majesty," Snow said.

He stood, but didn't dare look up at her. He did give Aidan a quick nod. The White Stag's eyes were wide, his jaw tense. Why wouldn't he be nervous, watching his ally and mentor leave him in a situation that Snow was supposed to be there to guide him through?

His heart was heavy as he walked from the throne room. Once more, he had disappointed his Queen. Worse, Aidan and Sylvia were left to navigate this tricky situation on their own. Snow had at least prepared his seneschals for such an eventuality, but he had thought it an unlikely scenario.

His steps were slow as he ascended the steps that would lead him outside of the castle. This wasn't the start Aidan and Sylvia deserved. Most of all, he hated the feeling that he had failed them.

—

Don't worry, the Krampus is definitely due his own happy ending, and the ride there will be epic! The journey resolves in the final book of the trilogy, *The Krampus*. You'll find links to many distributors for the book on my website at ***https://cassandra-chandler.com/the-krampus/***

For more of my Paranormal Romances, check out ***The Summer Park Psychics*** or ***Forbidden Instinct***. If you want to explore my other stories, you can go on out of this world adventures with the fated soulmates of the ***Cygnian 7*** series or check out short, steamy Sci-Fi Romances on a near-future Earth in that same universe with ***The Department of Homeworld Security***. And if you'd like a little bit of Scifi mixed into your Paranormal Romance, check out the ***Blades of Janus***.

I'd love to keep in touch. Join my newsletter at

sendfox.com/cassandrachandler to hear about all the adventures happening in Cassland. And if you enjoyed this book, please consider leaving a review at your favorite book review site. Reviews are so important to authors. You can also help by spreading the word among your friends. I appreciate you so much!

Thank you for reading *The White Stag!*

Cassandra Chandler

About the Author

USA Today Bestselling author Cassandra Chandler uses her vivid imagination to make the world more interesting, spawning the ideas she turns into her evocative Science Fiction Romances and enthralling Paranormal and Urban Fantasy Romances. Fast-paced and funny, lighthearted or tinged with shadow, her stories will introduce you to characters you'll fall in love with and worlds you long to explore.

www.ingramcontent.com/pod-product-compliance
Lightning Source LLC
Chambersburg PA
CBHW072228190626
46809CB00017B/1527